J A C K

Martin J. Roddini

Dedication

To the memory of my sister who worried that our relationship would change if I knew how we were truly related; and to my brother, who others, for self-serving reasons, portrayed him as my cousin. I miss you both.

Also by Martin J. Roddini

Saving Kings

They Can Hear

The Apparition

Jack

Chapter One

Jimmy Benson

He was born on the west side of Manhattan in the shadow of Peter Stuyvesant High School from which he would have liked to ultimately graduate. Both of his parents were born in Italy, and they carried the culture and norms of the Italian way of life to New York. Carmela and Antonio spoke little English but were able to get along well enough to raise three sons and five daughters. Carmela was the typical Italian mother who managed the household and the children while excelling in the culinary arts. Everything she created was an outstanding combination of meats, vegetables, and herbs. There were no specific measurements, just an estimation of what should be added to the simmering solution. This was the dictum for weekday evening meals, but on the weekends, it would be a combination of pasta and a variety of Italian seasoned meats swimming in a huge pot of tomato sauce. But no matter what combination of spices and herbs, and what variety of meats and pasta, Carmela always created a masterpiece of Italian culinary delight.

As Carmela had a background involving an ordinary upbringing in Italy, Antonio enjoyed a focused childhood that was above average. His demeanor and character actually demonstrated this difference. His education included graduation from high school and an acceptance into a specialized school where emphasis on the sea was the main theme. Antonio learned as much as he could about commercial shipping and ultimately applied this knowledge to his position as a merchant marine. Contrary to Carmela, his appearance and stature exuded an air of excellence and professionalism. Following his marriage to Carmela, he brought this calling with him to the United States, settling in New York City. It was there, in downtown Manhattan in sight of the West Side Highway, that three of the children, including Dominic their first son, was born.

Antonio quickly adapted to the American way of life and made numerous friends in and around the New York City dock area. His son, Dominic, who always seemed to be with him, became a recognizable figure to many of the workers. As a result of his background and education, Antonio quickly rose to a pseudo leadership role on the docks. He was well respected by the workers and the hierarchy who ran the operation at the port; and therefore, his son, Dominic had free run of the dock area.

The docks were unofficially operated by individuals who could be described as having underworld ties. They controlled what came into the port, when it was unloaded and who was hired to work the cargo. The weekdays were a very busy time on the docks, but on the weekends, the atmosphere was one of relaxation and friendship. The managers frequented the docks on weekends, and everything from barbeques to betting took place. One of the favorite betting pastimes involved Antonio's son, Dominic. Nature had gifted Dominic with the ability to run like the wind. Everyone seemed to know about this ability, and the skill became a talent that the managers would wager on.

The street under the West Side Highway was peppered with traffic lights on every corner. The betting game included a specific car and Dominic. Seeing a red light, the person betting on Dominic would point out a car and stipulate that the 10-year-old boy could outrun the car to the next corner. Dominic was that fast, and the betting went on throughout the day with the runner getting a certain percentage of the winnings. It was all done within the framework of a friendly wager and everyone, including Dominic, enjoyed it. This particular exercise only brought Antonio closer to the operators who managed the docks. He was becoming one of those people who could control certain operations on the docks. He slowly but surely was reaching that plateau where others looked to him for direction.

Having moved up the leadership scale, Antonio was able to realize enough money to move out of Manhattan and buy a house in the beautiful suburb of Brooklyn. This would be where he and Carmela would raise the rest of the family who were soon to be on their way. Carmela and Antonio had eight children all together. Dominic had two brothers: Frank and Michael, and they had five sisters: Mary, Eileen, Frances, Carol, and Alice. It was a large family, but nothing out of the ordinary for Italians who migrated to the United States. In a relatively short time, Antonio had come a long way to be able to comfortably support such a large clan. Because of his present position at the docks, he was demanding good money, he was respected, and most of all, he was feared.

In the Italian family, the oldest son was given certain responsibilities and obligations that the others might not even be privy to. And in Antonio's family, this weight and privilege fell to Dominic. It was rare that one would see Antonio walking in the Bensonhurst area of Brooklyn without his young son, Dominic, in tow. Although still young, Dominic learned more and more about his father's commitments every day. He knew that certain areas were off limits to him. He was charged with listening and learning, and he realized that some of his father's obligations included actions that sometimes rose to the point of possible violence and/or persuasion. This was emphatically demonstrated one early morning when Dominic accompanied his father on a routine walk to the candy store around the corner from their home. It was Antonio's habit to walk to the store every morning to purchase the morning paper. Dominic didn't mind this walk at all since it usually resulted in his getting a favorite candy bar.

As Dominic and his dad were leaving the candy store, and after Antonio had spoken with the owner for a period of time, as he usually did, they heard the squealing of automobile tires as a car turned the corner. Directly across the street from where Dominic and his dad were standing, they saw Jimmy Benson (short for Bensonhurst) staring at the speeding auto. The vehicle was occupied by four individuals, two of which were holding something outside of the opened windows. Suddenly, the stagnant air of Bensonhurst was penetrated by the reverberation of something that resembled the blasts that Dominic associated with a cherry bombs. However, the blasts were quick and louder than a firework, and it lasted for as long as the car passed by. When the car had finally passed out of view, Dominic saw the man across the street staggering and holding on to the front fence of the house where he had been standing. His white shirt was splattered with red stains that were growing by the second. The man's grip on the fence faltered, and he fell to the ground with a thud. He didn't move. All this happened in seconds and Dominic was shocked at what he thought he saw. He turned to his father and said: "Dad, did you see that? What just happened? Should we go across the street and help that man?"

"Son, you didn't see anything at all. Nothing happened here today. We just got the paper. You got your candy bar, and we had a nice conversation with our friend, Mr. Giantino. There was nothing to see."

"But dad..." That's all that Dominic got out when he saw the frightening and serious face of his dad who said, "Did you hear what I just said?"

Dominic understood not to say anything else. The whole event was Dominic's introduction to the world where his father had thrived and excelled. Dominic always had suspicions, but now he was convinced. His dad was involved in some way in the workings of the violent and corrupt arena where "survival of the fittest" was the mantra that all who played in that sphere lived by. His convictions now confirmed, Dominic looked at his father in a different light. He still loved him, respected him, and followed him, but now, he was also in fear of his father's potential for harm.

Chapter Two

The Garment Industry

Antonio's family prospered in their new home in the borough of Brooklyn. Even though Dominic now lived in a different borough, he traveled to Manhattan every day so that he could remain in Stuyvesant High School. He had made a lot of friends, and he was comfortable being a Stuyvesant student. His days were long as he combined his academic schedule with the sports program which included heavy participation on the track team. In fact, Dominic broke and set new track records for Peter Stuyvesant High School. He was a racing phenomenon. Unfortunately, because of family pressure and circumstances beyond his control, Dominic was unable to graduate. He left high school at the end of his junior year. He never finished his education and never received a diploma for graduation. However, Dominic was an intelligent and knowledgeable individual who was super sharp in mathematics. He amazed his parents and his siblings with his ability to quickly solve math problems that boggled the minds of others. It was this mathematical acumen that was attractive to local criminal operators who ran gambling and numbers games. Much to the dismay of his father, Dominic became involved in this illegal activity where he earned more money than any of his friends.

Time passed quickly, and Antonio saw how his son was getting too involved in the illegal workings of the local gambling operators. He decided to curtail his son's involvement in this unorthodox manner of making money because he knew that this introductory involvement into the activities of the underworld would surely lead to bigger and better opportunities. However, opportunities that surely came with higher risks and ultimately potentially higher punishment, if caught. So, Antonio made it his business to contact a close acquaintance of his who was well known in the garment industry. He convinced his friend to allow Dominic to begin a career in that industry.

Dominic had liked what he was doing, and more so, liked the income that he saw every week. So, to say the least, he was not happy when his father told him that arrangements had been made for him to begin a career in the clothing industry. Firstly, he knew nothing about that industry, and secondly, he had to start at an entry-level position which meant that the amount of money that he would receive at the end of the week would be considerably less than what he had been getting. However, there was no way that Dominic was going to challenge his father. Antonio had made the decision, and Dominic had no choice but to follow his father's "suggestion." Dominic had no way of knowing that this turn of events would only help him to become a productive member of the workforce where he could make a very good salary and learn an important commercial skill.

Dominic started his new job on a Monday morning in the beginning of July. He traveled to Manhattan on the subway which was always jammed with people who were angry at the world and who hated their jobs. Dominic was stunned with the sudden realization that he now fit perfectly into that group. He had no choice, so he had to make the best of it, but he hoped that his father would soon come to his senses. However, that was not to be. Dominic was welcomed to the world of garment production by the owner of a manufacturing company called "Belle Lingerie." The owner, Mr. Saul Levine, introduced himself and escorted his new employee to the packing and shipping department. This would be Dominic's new home for quite a while. Dominic knew that his father would probably never change his mind, so he decided to make lemonade out of lemons. He decided to watch and learn the different aspects of garment production from laying out the goods, to applying the patterns and to actually cutting the individual garments. He was not going to be relegated to the shipping department for the rest of his time in the industry.

Dominic had to start at the beginning. The manager of the shipping department took him under his wing, and, before long, Dominic became an integral part of the successful operation of the Belle Lingerie Shipping Department. His attention to detail and determination to follow a project to completion did not go unnoticed by management. It was also obvious that Dominic was interested in other areas of the business production. He could often be seen after hours talking to the cutters, fabric spreaders, and pattern makers picking their brains on the particular aspects of their positions. After a while, there were times when the skilled workers allowed Dominic to apply his observations to the actual creation of a specific piece or clothing. They were amazed at how well Dominic applied his observed knowledge to practical execution.

Dominic worked for Saul Levine for almost three years, and during that time he learned an awful lot about the business. With the unofficial okay of the skilled workers, Dominic did everything from laying the goods to actually cutting the garment according to pattern specifications. It was no surprise that when a position opened up in another shop, Mr. Levine recommended Dominic for the position. It was an introductory position to actually cutting garments. Although it would not be on the major production line, Dominic would be cutting model garments for inspection and appraisal and possible modification. The pay was a major boost in earnings, and Dominic was on his way to making a definite mark in the garment industry.

While Dominic was totally involved in the production market, his siblings were involved in a number of other areas. Frank, who was just a year or so younger than Dominic, followed in the original footsteps of his brother. He started working for people who operated just outside the limits of the law. Frank enjoyed the camaraderie that he shared with others who were also delving into illegal operations. Additionally, Frank also liked the increased monetary rewards gained by his cooperation in the efforts of those who were managers in this dark operation. Frank also had a different personality than his brother. He liked the excitement, the macho of the managers and what the future could possibly hold for him. Knowing that his father would not approve of his venture, Frank kept his work environment a total secret from Antonio. He also pleaded with his bosses to maintain secrecy. They agreed not to inform Antonio, but said that if they were asked, they would not lie about it. That was good enough for Frank.

As Dominic pushed forward in the garment industry, Frank pushed ahead with the mob. He was committed to rising up in the world of illicit transactions. His tough guy persona melded well into the mix of criminal activities. However, before Frank could actually realize his goal of moving up in the organization, there were certain initial steps that had to be successfully completed before a rise to a more meaningful position was possible. It was sort of an initiation into the mob. What did this mean for Frank? He would have to show that he was not afraid to take some risks for the benefit of the organization. He would have to get down and dirty and be willing to take a bigger leap over the line of legality. He would have to become a criminal.

As previously mentioned, Frank's personality differed greatly from that of his brother, Dominic. Frank had no problem working with others to steal, assault, or rob according to what was deemed necessary. It would take a long series of minor crimes before he would be looked upon as a potentially significant figure in the society of the underworld.

In stark contrast to both of his brothers, Michael, the youngest brother, was more laid back and looked to lead a simple but fulfilling life. He attended mass every week and enjoyed interacting with the church congregation. He volunteered much of his time to help out with church sponsored events and even became a lay deacon to distribute communion on Sundays. He had none of the ambition or determination that both of his brothers possessed, and since he was the youngest brother in an Italian family, he was more or less "babied." That having been said, however, there was nothing that Michael would not do for either Dominic or Frank. They were his brothers, and they never let him forget it. Conversely, both Dominic and Frank felt a certain responsibility in protecting their younger brother.

The girls in the family were all geared to becoming wives and mothers. They followed their mother's example and learned everything they could about managing a home. Their mom, Carmela, could cook, sew, administer needed medicine, and counsel her daughters on the facts of life. This sat well with all the girls except the youngest, Alice, who obviously had a mind of her own. She was going to be just as successful as her brothers. She did not want to know how to cook or sew. She wanted to be so successful that she could hire others to complete the tasks needed for the efficient operation of a household. Since her brother, Dominic, solidified a decent position in the garment industry, she decided to use him and hang onto his coattails to break into that industry.

In the family, Alice was looked upon as a rebel; however, in the work world she hoped that she would be looked at as an innovator, a new and productive participant in the garment industry. Mostly, she wanted to be recognized as someone who brought forth the birth of a brand-new way to look at fashion – a view from an innovative woman's perspective.

Chapter Three

A New Family Leader

Dominic was now a full-fledged garment worker. He was cutting samples that pattern makers were creating. He couldn't be happier with the way things worked out. In addition to the increased wages, he had gained the trust of his new boss and was respected as a worker who paid strict attention to detail. In the garment industry, that was a must.

Dominic was also aware that his sister, Alice, had taken specific courses geared to the fashion industry. He had put in a good word for her with his former boss, Saul Levine, and Alice was successful in getting a position as an assistant to the pattern maker. This was an ideal situation for Alice because she was able to closely follow the procedural steps in creating a new pattern or design. This, after all, is the area in which Alice was striving to excel. Once one is recognized as a designer or pattern maker, the garment world opens its doors to you. And if your designs are appealing to the masses, you can name your own ticket and start your own line of fashion. Alice felt that she was well on her way to achieving her goal. She was not going to be that happy housewife that her sisters were limiting themselves to. No, she was going to be a name that was recognized by all in the fashion world. She wanted her own line of clothes, her own shop and most of all, her own identity. No one was going to stand in her way, not her sisters, her brothers or even her father. She was her own person and was going to remain that way.

His family was getting older, and Antonio could no longer operate as he once did. He was still well respected in the business, but his overall role in the organization was somewhat limited. He, of course, still ruled his family with an iron fist, and everything had to be approved through him, but he had less and less influence over the decisions that the family, as a whole, had to make. In fact, he knew less and less about what had to be decided. He spent a good majority of his day walking with his dog down to the Brooklyn dock area. He was easily recognizable with his business suit and pocket watch hanging from his vest. He had a good relationship with the workers, and they enjoyed his company. The workers admired him for a number of reasons, not the least of which was the fact that he walked thirteen avenue blocks every day from his home to the waterfront, and he walked those same thirteen blocks back to his home at the end of the day. It looked like his dog was more tired than he.

Since Frank's association with the mob kept him, for the most part, close to home, he assumed the role of the unofficial head of the family. Although this role should have fallen to Dominic, he had no problems in allowing his younger brother to take the reins. Dominic was too involved with his work projects to devote the time needed to guide the family. So, by default, the siblings looked to Frank, most of the time, for guidance. And it was Frank who was bringing home those necessities of life and a variety of objects that the family never thought they would see. No one questioned where or how Frank obtained these resources that most families did not have. However, getting these "necessities" brought Frank deeper and deeper into the web of illegal activities. Frank felt, as most of the individuals involved in organized crime did, that he would never get caught. He was too smart for that. He unabashedly enjoyed the rewards from the illicit operations of which he had become an integral part.

Antonio's family was thriving and both the males and females in the family were doing exactly what they wanted. In fact, as the family grew and thrived, the predictable socialization process brought the siblings down different paths. Three of the five sisters had boyfriends, Dominic met someone who, in his opinion, could be the right one to spend the rest of his life with, and Frank had not one, but many girlfriends. Alice, who marched to the beat of a different drum, cast everything aside except for her goal to have her own fashion line operating out of her own shop. She cared very little for the social scene. She was solely focused on her work.

The family's real first setback occurred when they found their mom, Carmela, non-responsive in her bed. Unfortunately, Carmela unexpectedly had died in her sleep. This was a great blow to everyone in the family, but it was devastating for Antonio who had lost his life-partner. For the first time in his life, he did not know what to do. He had the comfort of his eight children, but he still felt totally alone.

As was expected, Frank took charge and arranged for the wake and the interment of his mother. As the mourners filed into the funeral home, one could say that it was the "Who's Who" of the local "connected" wannabes. Surely, the other siblings had friends and acquaintances who were there to offer their sympathies, but it seemed like the majority of people attending the wake were those who had some sort of relationship with Frank. Additionally, the funeral home director had to open an additional room just for the floral arrangements sent from these unsavory characters. It became the typical scene that one would see in a movie involving the mob and the loss of an individual close to a mob member.

It took his mother's death and her wake for Dominic to realize how deeply involved his brother, Frank, was in the organized crime world. He took this opportunity to call Frank to the side and have a pointed discussion about where his brother was heading. Out of respect for his older brother, Frank listened to Dominic until he could take it no more.

"Dominic, I have everything under control. Don't worry about me. I know what I'm doing."

"No, Frank. Apparently, you don't know what you're doing. If dad was himself, there is no way that you would continue to do the bidding for the crime family in which you are so seriously involved. For his sake, and frankly for your own good, bow out now before it's too late."

"Too late for what, Dominic. Because you didn't have the balls to follow through and make your way in the organization doesn't mean that I will do the same thing. I am well respected, making excellent money, and on the path to getting a chance to become a leader. There's no way that I give any of that up."

"Frank, you're not thinking straight. It's only good until it's not. There may very well come a day when things go wrong and before you know it, you're in court and convicted of a crime that will put you in prison. Who does that help? Your future will be ruined, and our family will be forever marked as associated with organized crime."

"Dominic, are you living in fantasy land? You and I both know that dad had connections to the mob. Sure, he may not have wanted you to get involved, but I'm sure we all benefited from his connections. So, don't be naive. People are aware of who dad is and how we exist in this competitive world. You take care of you, and I will take care of me. With all due respect, we never have to talk about this subject again."

Not giving his older brother a chance to speak again, Frank turned his back and walked away. Michael saw the heated exchange and went to Dominic to see if everything was okay. Dominic shook his head and just said that Michael should pray for his brother, Frank. Michael acknowledged Dominic's request and told him that he already prays for him every day.

There was no doubt in anybody's mind who was heading the family. Frank took control and never looked back. His father had very little to say about anything. As much as Antonio was involved in making certain that his oldest son did not join in with the mob, he had very little influence over the decisions that Frank made. Much to Antonio's disappointment, Frank was on the perimeter of the inner circle that formulated the leadership of the organized crime family. Frank was riding a wave that he hoped would bring him to the top. What he didn't consider was the fact that many individuals had ridden that same wave only to be wiped out by a strong undercurrent originating internally from envy and jealousy, and externally from law enforcement, arrest and prosecution. Very few were able to survive and escape the dangerous and ever-present undertow permeating the actions of the "family."

Chapter Four

Advice Not Taken

As time passed, the Balaticco family underwent a number of changes. The females were all involved with their partners, and two of the sisters were already married. The other two were close behind. The brothers had all followed different paths, and they too were examining the obligations connected to the matrimonial bonds.

Michael met a woman who was as involved in the church as he was, so their match was inevitable. They were obsessed with all things related to the church and church events. They had been with each other for a very long time, and they were not in a rush to complicate their lives with the responsibilities and obligations of marriage. The church approved of these long engagements, and they were not about to challenge the clear and authoritative thinking of the church. So, they stayed in this approved relationship and waited until the time was right. They were both celibate, and they agreed to only enhance their sexual relationship once they had the blessing of the church and God through the sacrament of matrimony. It was rare for a couple to abide by such stringent guidelines, but Michael and his fiancée agreed that they would follow the Christian way of life; and therefore, they would not culminate their relationship until they exchanged wedding vows at the altar.

Dominic was totally involved in the work environment. He found very little time to socialize and look for a life partner. He was happy devoting his time to bettering his chances in the industry and learning as much as he possibly could. When he did have some free time, he was just too tired to frequent the club and bar scene. So, it was somewhat of a miracle that he actually met a young woman to whom he was attracted, and someone who was apparently interested in him. She was about the same age as he but came from a very strict family. She had two siblings, both males, and therefore, she was responsible for many of the cleaning and household tasks. Men weren't assigned to do those sorts of things. If one didn't know better, one could assume that she would do anything to get out from under. However, it did seem that she had the same feelings that Dominic had when it came to their relationship. They met at an event that celebrated the merging of two companies. Marjorie was the daughter of one of the foremen associated with the company that Dominic's boss was acquiring.

For a good part of the celebration, Dominic and Marjorie spent time just talking to each other about their families. All during that time, however, Marjorie's father had one eye on his daughter and her new acquaintance. As previously stated, Marjorie lived under very strict guidelines. There was nothing that Marjorie could do, say, or even think about that was not first approved by her very overprotective, dictatorial father. She even hesitated mentioning anything about her family life to Dominic for fear that her father might find out. She requested and got a promise of strict confidentiality from Dominic before she let her hair down and unburdened herself by relating the constant parental fear that she lived under.

Her report of her hardships only strengthened the burgeoning feelings that were surfacing in Dominic's consciousness. The more she spoke, the more Dominic felt that his feelings were growing and that, at one point, because he cared so much for her, he would rescue her from a life that seemed almost unbearable. However, he guarded himself against reacting purely out of pity. If he was to spend the rest of his life with this woman, he had to make sure that his feelings were mounted in love and not in anything else. Although it seemed that they both hit it off rather well, he knew that the road to a final bond was going to be difficult, and he wanted to make certain that Marjorie's sentiments were also anchored in love. From that moment on, and much to the dismay of her father, Marjorie only dated Dominic.

While Michael was following the righteous path dictated by the church, and Dominic carefully negotiating his way around Marjorie's father and into her heart, the unofficial head of the family, Frank, was socializing whenever and wherever he could. Much of his free time was spent accepting invitations to various social clubs that were organized throughout the city, and much to his credit, these clubs boasted various ethnic backgrounds. Although he frequented Italian clubs more than others, he could be seen at events at Polish clubs, Spanish clubs, and Irish clubs. He was not a heavy drinker, but he often remarked that one could not beat the array of alcoholic beverages on display at an Irish club event. In fact, it was at one of these Irish social clubs where he met a young woman who commanded his attention.

Colleen knew one of the organizers associated with the Irish social club, so she attended many of the events. As soon as Frank saw her, he was attracted to the overall look. She seemed different than the others, and one could see that her fashion only accented her look. Frank had never dated an Irish woman, and he had no specific desire to do so. However, when he saw Colleen, he realized that maybe Irish was the way to go.

Although Frank was a demanding figure on the work scene, he was intelligent enough to know that a dictatorial figure was not one that was attractive to most women when it came to socializing. His approach was a careful, calculated, almost shy introduction, and for the most part, this approach had been successful. It was not at all a false pretense. Frank liked women, and most of all, he respected them. It was ingrained in him from his father who made sure that his sons treated all women as he had treated their mother. So, Frank was not a brute who demanded a female's attention, but rather a gentleman who appreciated the company of an accepting woman.

It was this non-intimidating, gentle attitude that appealed to Colleen when Frank introduced himself to her. They danced and spoke throughout the night, and Frank received an affirmative response from Colleen when he asked if he could call her sometime in the future. She gave him her phone number and told him that she hoped to speak to him soon.

Frank hadn't felt this way about any of the other women whom he dated. He was experiencing something new, and he liked it. He knew that he was going to face the harassment of his associates and friends when he introduced his Irish date to them, but he felt that it was well worth it. As he thought about it, none of the other guys were seeing anyone other than Italian women. This was the norm, but Frank was never a follower, he was a leader. So, it was natural for him to break the mold. He would soon, hopefully, be dating an Irish-American young woman.

Although Antonio was old, he had aged relatively well. He still had his wits about him and was very much attuned with what Frank had been doing. Antonio hadn't wanted any of his sons to get involved with an organized crime family, but

Frank's insertion and rise was much too quick for Antonio to have stopped it. So, he took the occasion one Sunday after dinner to tell Frank that he wanted to speak to him. Frank knew that his father had something on his mind just by the way he had been acting at dinner.

So, shortly after dinner, Antonio and Frank went into the living room and sat down to talk. However, unbeknownst to Frank, Antonio had invited Dominic to be a part of the meeting. Although Frank was a little taken aback by the sudden surprise, he said nothing and welcomed his older brother. It was understood that Antonio was technically still the head of the family, and whatever guidelines he dictated had to be accepted. Dominic nodded and sat down to join the conversation. Dominic understood his role to be one of mostly a listener, so that was the attitude he took.

When Antonio started speaking, he opened with the fact that he loved his children very much and only wanted the best for them. He then looked directly at Frank and said: "Frank, I do not know if what you are doing is the best for you. I'm sure you are aware of my association with some of the same people you now call friends, but I must warn you that they are friends to your face, but you can never turn your back on them."

This came out as a warning that Frank didn't expect. However, he realized that his father was not yet through expressing himself, so Frank just continued to listen without interruption.

"I was successful in stopping your brother Dominic from associating with these people, and I know that it is late, but I want you to consider leaving the group. I will help you find another area where you can excel and make money. You do not need the mob to dictate your future, and I worry that the future you are looking at is one that could only hurt you and the rest of our family. You are looking at the short-term benefits and not looking down the road at what the long-term problems may be. Get out now while you still can."

Frank understood that his father had finished speaking, and he took the opportunity to speak up: "Dad, thank you for your advice, and I know that you are always looking out for all of us, but I am too well situated in an organization that has only helped me and indirectly the entire family. There is no way that I can now leave, nor do I want to. I respect your advice and council, but I have been guiding our family, and I can only continue to do that If I remain where I am. It breaks my heart not to be able to follow your wishes but understand that I cannot."

There was a disturbing silence in the room, and it was only interrupted when Dominic, at the urging of his father, began to speak: "Frank, you are definitely not in that deep that you couldn't get out. You just don't want to leave. Use your head. You are jeopardizing your future and the good name of our family. Listen to dad, and I'm sure he can help after you make your decision."

Frank looked at his brother with fierce determination in his eyes. He rose from his chair and spoke directly to

Dominic: "Dominic, don't you ever tell me to use my head. I am the one who is supporting and guiding this family. I have that responsibility on my shoulders, not you. I told dad that I cannot follow his advice, and I am telling you to never attempt to advise me on my way of life. You know nothing about it. You had your chance, and you tiptoed out. I do not need you to be telling me anything!"

Dominic rose from his seat and was about to come back at his brother when Antonio yelled as best as he could: "Stop! The two of you are acting as if you are not my sons." As he struggled to rise from his chair, Antonio grabbed his chest and fell to the floor. He was breathing, but just barely.

Chapter Five

Don't Test Me

Antonio had suffered a heart attack but was doing well at the hospital. However, the relationship between Dominic and Frank remained strained. The tension affected the entire family, and it seemed that everyone was on edge. There was bickering among the sisters over the smallest things, and Frank's superior and dictatorial attitude was definitely rubbing Dominic the wrong way. Unfortunately, with Antonio in the hospital there was no mediator; no one to bring the parties together. It was taking its toll on everyone.

Dominic had always loved the sport of boxing. He had boxed a number of times in the local gym and had won a few bouts. To avoid any further conflict within the family, Dominic decided to turn his free time into a disciplined effort in the ring. So, after work each day, he headed to the gym to get in boxing shape once again. He didn't like taking time away from Marjorie, and so, she was more than willing, at times, to accompany him to the gym. His family also encouraged him to get back in the game. He worked hard, and before long, he was scheduled for a match with a local boxer who needed time in the ring. It was assumed that this match would just be an exhibition outing for the other boxer to get in shape; but to the surprise of many people, Dominic proved to be the victor. He not only won the match, but he knocked out his opponent. This result only encouraged him to continue competing in the ring.

Dominic was becoming a known entity in the local boxing venue, and for the sake of his family's reputation, he decided to box under the pseudonym of Jack Martin – a name that was suggested by his girlfriend. Jack was getting better and better as time went on, but he was facing fighters who were a lot younger than he. Jack had more experience, but others were in better shape and could last longer in the ring. Jack Martin continued to win, but the pounding on his body was beginning to take its toll on his overall health.

Watching Jack workout in the gym one day, a relatively young and new middleweight fighter was impressed with what he saw. He had heard a lot of good things about Jack Martin and had made a special trip to this gym just to meet him. Following Jack's work out, the middleweight, Matty Stevens, approached Jack and asked to speak with him. Jack had no problem speaking to the young boxer but asked him to wait until he finished showering and got dressed. Matty had no problem with waiting for Jack.

As soon as Jack came out of the locker room, he approached the young boxer who was waiting patiently for him.

"Hello there, as you know I am Jack Martin, and you are?"

"Glad to meet you Mr. Martin. I'm Matty Stevens, and I am a middle weight boxer."

"Before we start anything, the name is 'Jack.' Mr. Martin sounds like what people would call my father. Okay, so you are a middle weight boxer. What can I do for you?"

"Well, I've seen you fight, and I've studied some of the video. I would like to learn boxing technique from you. In a recent interview, you mentioned that you might be thinking about staying in the fight game, but outside of the ring. Mr. Martin, I mean Jack, I do not have a manager right now, and I would like to know if you would be interested in managing me."

"You're right, I did mention that I am considering something outside of the boxing ring, but I really didn't consider managing anyone. This comes as a total surprise, and I just don't know if I would be the right person for you. I've boxed, but I've never managed. Maybe, you should look for someone with managing experience."

"Jack, I want to learn from you. How better to learn than from my manager. I have weighed my other options, but I am convinced that you would be the best person for the job. I think I have what it takes to be a good boxer, but I need someone with your experience to help guide the way."

"Well, I appreciate the confidence that you have in me, Matty, but I wasn't expecting to leave the ring so soon. Tell you what. Let me think about it and do a little research on Matty Stevens, and I'll get back to you in a week's time. How does that sound?"

"Jack, I'll be waiting to hear from you, and I won't disappoint you."

Matty Stevens said his good-bye and left the gym. As soon as he left, the owner of the gym came over to Jack: "Hey, I couldn't help but hear some of your conversation with that young kid. I have heard his name before, and I only hear good things about him. He is a Brooklyn kid, and, from what I hear, he is determined to be a winner. This might be just the right thing for you. You're not getting any younger, and this way, you'll still have your finger in the pie. Leave while you still have a good reputation and people look up to you. Ride the kid's wave the rest of the way."

"I appreciate your input, Gus, but I just don't know if I'm ready to quit fighting. I'll have to think it over. I'm going to discuss it with my girlfriend and the rest of my family, and then make a decision."

"Jack, you have another whole life outside of boxing. Concentrate on that and take the kid's offer. Don't be foolish. You're fighting opponents who are a lot younger than you, and sooner or later, they are going to get to you. While you're still in one piece and have all your faculties, take the offer and run."

"Well, thanks for the strong vote of confidence. You make me feel that I can conquer the world! But you know, you just may be right. I'll give retirement some serious thought while I still have my faculties!"

With that last bit of sarcasm, Dominic (Jack Martin) left the gym and headed home where his girlfriend was meeting him for dinner with his family. Marjorie got along very well with all of Dominic's siblings. She enjoyed being with Jack's family because with them she didn't have to answer the thousand and one questions that her father would have asked her at the dinner table. Additionally, she enjoyed the Italian meals that the family always prepared. Not only was there plenty to eat, but there was a variety of Italian specialties that would rival the finest Italian restaurants. Marjorie's mother prepared good American dinners, but there was nothing like a good Italian feast.

When the dinner was over and just before dessert was served, Dominic saw the perfect opportunity to raise the question about his pugilistic future. He had no idea about what the consensus of opinion would be other than the fact that he knew Marjorie loved the idea that he was a boxer. He believed that her vote would be cast in stone and would be geared toward his remaining in the ring. However, he really had no idea what the rest of the family would say. He started his survey with the unalarming but hopefully attention getting phrase: "Well, I had a very interesting day today." He looked around, and the fact that he was standing and speaking aloud caught everyone by surprise, and therefore, demanded their attention.

"No, actually, I had an even more interesting afternoon. While I was sparing with one of the guys in the gym, a young man walked into the gym and unbeknownst to me was observing my sparing session. He waited until it was over and then approached me. He knew who I was, and he greeted me by name. He then introduced himself to me and asked if he could speak to me. I had no problem speaking to him, but I asked him to wait until I showered and came out of the locker room. He had no problem doing that."

In a joking but also serious manner, Alice asked: "Is there going to be an end to this story?" Everyone sort of smiled, but Dominic continued on with his comments: "When I finally got out of the locker room, the young man introduced himself again as Matty Stevens, a middle weight boxer. He further explained that he had observed me boxing in person and on tape and had heard that there was a possibility that I was considering taking a position outside of the ring itself. I acknowledged that I had said something relative to that. He then said that he did not have a manager and wondered if I would consider managing him. From all indications and from what I have been told, he is a very decent boxer and wants me to teach him my boxing technique. I didn't give him any answer and told him that I would think about it and that I would contact him in a week. So, here tonight, I am asking your opinion as to whether I should continue fighting in the ring or fighting like hell to get this middle weight boxer a shot at a title."

It was a lot for all of them to take in, and there was a deafening silence in the room. The first one to break the silence and give her opinion was Marjorie, and her response was exactly what Dominic thought it would be. She emphasized Jack Martin's success in the ring, and she felt that it was much too soon to retire from that successful venture. She used the name Jack Martin because she and the rest of his family got into the habit of calling him "Jack."

There was mumbling and indecipherable grumbling among the group when Michael stood up and commented in a way as to demonstrate that he represented the consensus of opinion.

"Jack, we are all so impressed with your boxing record, and we are proud of the way you have conducted yourself. We are sure that you could win more matches and rise in popularity, but we are also afraid that there may come a time when you sustain a serious injury. Of course, none of us want to see that. We are also aware that most of the boxers are younger than you, and that disadvantage could lead to a devasting injury. So, speaking for the rest of the group, although there are some differences of opinion, we feel that you should accept Matty Stevens offer and become his manager."

Marjorie was sorely disappointed, and she turned to Frank who was of the same opinion as she. Frank just shrugged his shoulders and whispered to her that, once again, Jack was taking the coward's way out. Unfortunately, the whisper was loud enough for everyone to hear, including Jack. Jack responded: "No, Frank, the coward is the one who has to hide behind the armor of organized crime because he can't stand alone." Frank rose in a fighting stance, and Jack just said: "You're out of your league. You don't want to test me!" Frank just looked around and left the house saying: "Fists won't ever stop a bullet!"

Chapter Six

The Contact Man

Alice wasn't sure that she heard what her brother had said. So, she asked: "Did Frank just say that fists won't ever stop a bullet." Knowing Alice, the way the group knew her, they were sure she knew what her brother had said but she wanted to repeat it for emphasis. She really couldn't believe that he said what he said, and she wasn't exactly sure what he meant by it. It could be interpreted in a number of ways, and one of those ways could surely indicate a threat to her brother, Jack.

Alice looked around the room in a questioning manner as to say, "Well, what do you all think?" At first, no one spoke up, but then Michael, the peacemaker, commented: "I am sure that Frank didn't mean anything by it. He was just hot under the collar. He has always looked out for the family, and I'm sure he will be doing that in the future." Michael then turned to Jack and spoke directly to him: "Nothing changes our opinion regarding your decision, Jack. We want you to be safe while remaining in the boxing world. Your managing Matty is the way to go."

As the rest of the family nodded their approval, there was one standout, Marjorie. She definitely wanted Jack to remain inside the ring. She knew that she would enjoy the personal gratification of being the wife of a respected boxer. She wasn't taking into account her soon-to-be husband's safety nor age, but just the fact that she would also be in the limelight. However, and much to her disappointment, the family had spoken, and Jack was going to follow their decision.

"I want you all to know that if I were a bit younger, there would be no way that I would leave the ring. But you are all right. Each time I step into the ring now, I take a chance that I could be seriously hurt. Additionally, I do not want to go out a loser, so leaving when one is on top is the way to go."

Marjorie couldn't stay quiet any longer: "Jack, you are underestimating yourself. You know that you are a good boxer, and everyone here knows it too. You are cutting short a career that could prove to be rewarding beyond expectation. I am your fiancé, and hopefully soon to be your wife. Don't you think that I would want what's best for you?"

Michael, who was usually very layback but seeing through Marjorie's comments, couldn't resist a response:

"Marjorie, with all due respect, it might be best for you, but we do not think it would be best for our brother."

After Michael's comment, Jack stepped in and ended any further conversation on the subject. He reiterated that he was going to follow the advice of his family, and that he would contact Matty Stevens to accept his offer. As soon as Jack ended his comments, Marjorie rose from her chair and left the room. No one was surprised by her actions because she was used to getting whatever she wanted from Jack. However, this time she had to compete with the decision of the family, who, for the most part, really liked her and sided with her most of the time.

Jack thanked everyone for their consideration and then went to look for Marjorie. He was aware that she enjoyed being in the winner's circle with Jack each time he was a victor. But he was concerned why she was so adamant about his continuing in the ring. As Michael had indicated, it seemed that she was more concerned about her own success rather than his health. He hadn't seen this side of her, and he just didn't understand it. He had to talk to her and get everything out in the open. If this was going to be the woman who he was going to marry, then he should know where her head is. He hoped that she wasn't intentionally hiding her true feelings from him. If she really loved him, wouldn't she be more concerned about his safety than her basking in the glory of his victories? Maybe, he was jumping the gun. He was sure that after he spoke with her, he would see a different attitude, and one that would show how much she cared for him.

When Frank left the house and his family, he regretted what had occurred. However, he could not let the challenge by his brother go unanswered, so he responded in the best fashion he could, with a threat. He did not want to do it, but his immediate reaction was one that showed his obvious connection to an organization that would stoop to any depth to win. After all, he was the unofficial head of his family, and he had to show the rest of his siblings and their partners that he was someone who should not be reckoned with. He was sure that he got his point across, but now, there was no stepping back from how he would lead.

Although he left in an unexpected manner that alarmed his family, the fact was that he had to leave anyway. One of the bosses of the organization wanted to meet with him to discuss a new venture that could be financially rewarding for the crime family and for him. He viewed this as a step up. He was going to be the contact person for the crime family. So, although he left his house before he really intended to, it served the purpose of getting to the meeting in plenty of time. It showed his enthusiasm and respect for all that was organization oriented.

Frank was no stranger to the city, and he was going to meet one of the managers at a location that was not far from his family's old stomping grounds near Stuyvesant High School. It was a storefront that sold a variety of restaurant equipment, and in the back room was a conference table, phones, a television, an arrangement of comfortable chairs, and a fully equipped ready-to-use kitchen with a refrigerator and stove.

Frank was too early to actually enter the store, so he waited patiently parked outside and in view of the entrance. He wanted to show that he was enthusiastic about any new venture, but he didn't want anyone to believe that he was overly excited about an operation. To the family, that might be a sign of weakness, and that was the last thing that he wanted to convey.

At approximately ten minutes before meeting time, Frank exited his car and walked to the store. As soon as he entered, he was approached by a man whose physical anatomy would have filled any doorway. But Frank, putting on his game face, stayed his ground and asked for the individual with whom the meeting was scheduled. He was escorted to the back-room entrance where he was patted-down for weapons. Having been cleared, the escort opened the door and announced Frank's presence. Frank entered the room where he saw a tall but stocky individual, standing over the stove. The man was stirring something inside of a pot and never turned to look at Frank. The man, Anthony (Tony) Delfiato, told Frank to take a seat at the table, and that he would be right with him.

Frank now knew what the man had been stirring because the entire room smelled of tomato sauce. It brought a smile to Frank's face because it reminded him of the many Sundays when his mom's house smelled the same way. It served to calm some of the nervous feeling that had settled in Frank's stomach. Shortly, the man left the stove and came to the table where Frank was sitting.

"You know, you have to keep stirring the sauce so that it doesn't burn. Nothing worse than burned tomato sauce."

Frank just nodded politely and waited for the man to continue. There were protocols when one was in the presence of a ranking family member. Frank followed those protocols and waited through the pregnant pause.

"Frank, in case you didn't know, I am Tony Delfiato, and I manage a number of things for the organization. I am presently involved with starting a new operation, and I am in need of a man who can act as our contact. Your name came up at a meeting where this new venture was being discussed. If you are the right man for the job, I think it will be most beneficial for the family as well as for you personally. I am aware of your father's past involvement, and it is with that background in mind that I asked you here today. Are you ready to help out with the progress of the business needs of our organization?"

"Absolutely, Mr. Delfiato. Whatever you need."

"That's the right answer, Frank. We are going to have a future meeting where we will get further into the operation, but for now, I needed to know if we would have your full cooperation. I am going to assume that you will be our contact with the others involved in the operation. As long as there are no objections from the others who know about the venture, consider yourself as being an integral part of what we all hope will be a more than a rewarding experience. Speak to no one about this, whether that individual is inside or outside our organization, and that includes Antonio."

Tony got up from the table to once again begin stirring the sauce. He turned and looked at Frank and said: "Is there something bothering you? I have nothing more to say. So, if you have nothing to add, I will be in touch with you. There's the door."

Frank was unceremoniously told to leave. He understood that it was the mob way, but he was still taken aback. But he was not a friend of Tony's, he was someone who Tony was going to utilize to help with a business venture, and that was all he was. He accepted that.

When Frank reached his car, he mentally reviewed the entire meeting. There was only one thing that bothered him. Tony Delfiato made it a point to tell him not to discuss anything with his father. He wondered why he couldn't tell his father who had been involved for many years with the workings of the family. Tony either didn't trust Antonio or worse, he thought that Antonio would try to squash the operation to save his son. Frank started to wonder about the risks that would be involved. The words of his brother, Jack, and his father, Antonio, came rushing into his consciousness, and those words implied that an association with the mob would only end with prison or even death. Now, instead of enthusiasm, Frank started feeling the effects of emotions that were new and totally foreign to him – anxiety and fear.

Chapter Seven

No Compromise

The decision was made, and Jack contacted Matty Stevens to tell him that he had a new manager. In addition to Jack's decision, the Antonio family was making many other decisions. Two of the three women had set the date for their wedding, and two others had recently accepted an engagement ring. However, when it came to the romantic scene, there was one holdout. Alice was consumed with getting on with her business ventures and becoming a leader in the newly established arena of women's fashion. She was well on her way to reaching her goal, and any possibility of a romantic connection took a back seat.

Even Michael, who was closely involved in the everyday operation of the church, was entertaining the idea of getting serious about a romantic partnership and the possibility of raising a family. He was already engaged, but there had been no talk about a wedding day. Now, his fiancé, Denise, was hinting toward making their relationship a permanent one. Michael apparently did not have any objection to setting a wedding day. So, they too were in the family circle of getting on with their lives.

As Frank became more involved with organized crime, he also became more involved with his girlfriend, Colleen. He surprised Colleen with a large diamond ring and asked her to marry him. There was no hesitation on her part, and they both quickly set a wedding date. So, other than Alice, the only other family member who had not set a date for marriage was Jack. He had apparently let Marjorie down when he made a decision to follow his family's advice. So, in an effort to make things right, Jack Martin asked Marjorie to marry him. It seemed that Marjorie couldn't have been happier. She immediately accepted Jack's proposal and told him that she didn't want to wait for any length of time to get married. She had indicated that the faster they got married the better it would be. Jack wanted to get married, but he didn't want to rush into it; however, that wasn't his decision. Marjorie relentlessly pressured him into setting a date that was in the very near future. Again, feeling somewhat guilty regarding his decision to manage rather than box, he went along with Marjorie's wishes, and they set a date that was quickly approaching.

The Antonio family was growing by leaps and bounds. With everyone getting engaged or married, Antonio's influence over the happenings in the family were reduced to respectful introductions. As he got older, all Antonio wanted was respect, and everyone in the family, including the new additions, gave him that deference. His sons and daughters never failed to include him in decisions that were being made. They included him, but his opinion, although often considered, was never the deciding factor in the final outcome. His involvement was mostly routine.

Jack met with Matty Stevens for their first training session in the gym. Jack was impressed with Matty's training regimen and immediately had a good feeling about his decision. He would show this young boxer all he could about the fight game and work with him to concentrate on a good life inside and outside of the ring. He was not going to let this young contender get involved in the undercurrent of boxing where many a decent fighter floundered into mediocrity by taking their eye off the prize, the respect of all who participated in the game.

Matty had stamina and strength, both of which were great assets in the ring. He listened carefully to whatever Jack said and treated him with the respect given to a champion. Jack Martin was not a champion, but he had been successful in the majority of his matches. Jack's technique was a little different than that of other boxers, and this is what drew Matty to offer him a manager's position. Their relationship was more than a manager and a boxer. It was developing into a younger and older brother situation, one with which Jack was quite familiar.

Matty Stevens, under the tutelage of Jack Martin, had thus far competed in eight fights. He was successful in all eight, winning six of the eight with a knockout punch. This show of power caught the attention of a number of boxing aficionados who took more than a passing interest in this relatively new boxer. In fact, they were so interested in Matty Stevens that they approached the boxer after one of his matches. Luckily for him, Jack was not there at the time, and Matty put them off with the fact that he had to speak to his manager before he considered any offer made by the visitors.

When Jack Martin heard from Matty that he had been approached by some businessmen about his future, Jack was both livid and concerned. He explained to his phenom that these individuals were more than businessmen. They were part of an organization that would not take "no" for an answer. As Matty listened carefully, Jack told him how the offer would work. Matty Stevens would become their fighter, and they would take a part of whatever winnings came his way. Sure, they would arrange for larger venues and bigger purses, but he would no longer have any say in what was scheduled. Jack also warned Matty that there was a good possibility that the time would come when he would be asked to do something that would benefit the benefactors but hurt him as a boxer. He explained that "throwing a fight" was definitely a possible request that they might make of him. Jack also explained that the word "request" should be interpreted as a dictum that if not followed would result in dire consequences.

Jack Martin knew these types of businessmen. They had very little interest in the fight game but a determined stake in the monetary benefits of the final outcome. Jack was definitely trying to enlighten Matty regarding involvement with organized crime figures, and he was also trying to scare him into refusing any association with the underworld. Jack was successful in doing both, but the problem now was how to decline the offer without experiencing what could amount to a situation where possible physical harm could be utilized to influence a positive acceptance.

Although Jack hated to do it, he had only one option, and that was to speak to his brother, Frank, and ask for help. Jack told Matty that he would handle everything. Jack reached out to his brother, who, at first, was reluctant to even speak to Jack. Frank had become more involved with the crime family and was recognized as someone who got things done. Jack explained the situation to his brother and asked for help in getting people off his back. Frank explained to Jack that what he was asking was not easily done, but he told him that he would look into it. Jack hated to go to Frank for help, but for the sake of his young friend, he had no choice. Frank threw a couple of jabs into the conversation, and Jack had to swallow some humble pie. But he was willing to do that if Frank could use his influence to stop what could be a devastating blow to Matty Stevens' successful rise in the fight game.

Jack met with Matty and told him that he had someone working on the situation. The young boxer looked relieved and went on to win his next four fights. Just before the first round of Matty's next fight, Frank and another individual came into the locker room where Matty Stevens was preparing for the fight. Frank introduced his associate as Freddie. He explained to both Jack and Matty that Freddie would be meeting with them both to discuss the compromise that had been reached. Although Matty Stevens would have to give a certain percentage to Freddie, Matty would not be owned by anyone in the organization. Jack knew that there had to be some sort of compromise, and he thought that this was the best that they could hope for. The fact that Matty would remain a "free" boxer was a big win for the Jack Martin team. However, the specific percentage package could be a big factor in Matty never becoming financially stable. Jack thanked Frank and they shook hands. Freddie just nodded.

It was settled that Jack and Matty had to turn over twenty-five percent of all winnings to Freddie, and it was understood that any miscalculations could result in penalties from which neither Jack nor Matty would recover. This arrangement went on for a number of fights, and although the parties had agreed to the guidelines, Freddie never seemed happy about the situation, which meant that his bosses were not happy either. Sure, because of Frank's intercession, a compromise had been reached, but it just didn't sit well with the organization. Because of Frank, the crime family tolerated the situation.

Following another successful match, where the purse was larger than usual, Matty invited his manager to dinner at a local steak house. Jack accepted the invitation and told Matty that he would wait for him in his car across the street from the arena. Matty showered and hurried to meet Jack outside. As he exited the athletic hall, Matty saw Jack parked across the street. He started to cross the street when, out of nowhere, a car approached at high speed. Jack, who was involved in reading a fight report, heard the screeching of tires. As he turned toward the noise, he saw Matty Stevens flying through the air, the apparent victim of a hit and run accident. Jack ran to Matty as the young boxer laid there bleeding, life ebbing from him. Matty Stevens died in the street outside of the boxing arena that had just announced his victory.

The crime family was never really happy with the compromise. It became quite obvious that the word "compromise" didn't really exist in the organized crime lexicon. Jack Martin knelt in the street and cried.

Chapter Eight

The Surprise and the Operation

The incident with Matty Stevens hit Jack Martin very hard. He wanted nothing more to do with boxing or the fight game. He was doing well in the garment industry and concentrated solely on excelling in it. He was now a "cutter" which meant that he was actually forming the shape of the garments to be produced. He operated a number of different cutting machines and was quite effective with all of them. Jack was seen as one of those operators who meticulously paid attention to detail which is one of the traits that makes for a good production result. His efficiency and effectiveness helped in saving and reducing production costs, which was the paramount interest for the manufacturer. So, Jack became a favorite of the owners, and he was given those assignments that others would shy away from. The boss and others looked at Jack as an official lead in the actual production of a garment. This trust and his reputation ultimately led to Jack being touted as a potential foreman in a shop.

Unfortunately, the foreman's position was filled in the shop where Jack currently worked, but a foreman's position opened up in a shop closely associated with the one in which he presently operated. Although his boss didn't relish the thought of losing Jack, he did encourage Jack to apply for the position. Jack liked where he worked, so he applied for the position with mixed emotions. However, with his boss's endorsement, Jack was a shoo-in for the position. Shortly after he applied and went for an interview, Jack was notified that he was going to be the foreman at "Allure Lingerie." This was definitely a step up for Jack, and the increase in pay would make his new bride very happy.

Marjorie was a materialistic individual and very unhappy when she wanted something but could not afford it. Jack had to ride herd on her potential for unchecked spending. Sure, Jack was going to see an increase in salary, but it wasn't going to be so great as to eliminate all of the financial burdens that young married couples had.

When Jack arrived home from work with the good news regarding his new job, he was also greeted with news. Marjorie had made an appointment with her doctor who informed her that she was pregnant. This news took the wind out of the sails regarding Jack's news. Now, he needed the extra money to support a growing family. So, instead of having some additional funds to offset the ever-growing expenses of everyday living, Jack and Marjorie were mandated to watch their spending even more carefully than before. Although Marjorie's contribution to the family budget was minimal, it would be gone when the baby arrived. Jack was sure that Marjorie would insist on being a stay-at-home mom, so there would be no other monies other than what Jack brought home.

By all means, Jack was happy to hear that he was going to be a father, but his happiness was tempered with the knowledge that supporting a wife and a child was no easy task. However, all he showed Marjorie was the joy that accompanied the announcement that a baby was soon to arrive. Both Marjorie and Jack wanted to be surprised regarding the baby's gender, so they did not inquire about it. Marjorie was so happy just to be out of her father's dictatorial reach that the news of her pregnancy was the cherry on top of her new found freedom. Though she rarely showed Jack that she was happy to be with him, she was overjoyed to share her life with the new addition.

Jack's announcement to the rest of the family was greeted with unrestrained excitement. Marjorie was well liked in the family, and she was going to have the first baby out of all the romantic relationships that had been formed. From the point of the announcement to the day of the actual birth, Marjorie was coddled by everyone in the family. She could do no wrong, and she was granted the majority of her wishes. The fact that Jack was going to be the father was pushed to the back burner by the largely female family contingent. Instead of him becoming the flag bearer of the family crest, he was relegated to what seemed like just an insignificant element that was needed for the event to take place.

Jack took his new and better paying position in stride and worked extra hard to earn as much money as he could. In addition to his foreman position, he worked a second job as a cutter on weekends. Slowly but surely, he was putting money away to combat the new expenses that he and his wife would incur as the family expanded. For no other purpose other than to make sure that monies were there when they were needed, Jack kept a separate account that would not be touched until the baby arrived. He did this because he knew that his wife would spend these funds if she knew about them. He did not like being secretive, but Marjorie would be pleasantly surprised when he showed her the account after nine months. She would be relieved that they had monies that were there for the needs of their baby.

While Jack worked extra hard to save for the baby's arrival, his brother, Frank, was working hard to rise up on the mob ladder. He had heard from Tony Delfiato, and attended a meeting that Tony set up with two other associates with whom Frank would be working. The meeting was a no-nonsense, straight-to-the-point type huddle. The two individuals were introduced as Sal and Joe. There were no last names given, and Frank was smart enough not to ask.

Frank was told that he would be working very closely with the two, and that they would supply the information that was needed to conduct the operation.

As Frank listened carefully to what Tony was saying, he kept looking at the two individuals who were seated across from him. They just didn't look like the typical mob figures that Frank had been used to seeing, if there was such a thing as a typical mob figure, and they were both dressed in business suits. As Frank was sizing them up, so too were they evaluating their new contact.

When Tony finished with his explanation of the operation and his emphatic warning regarding confidentiality, Sal had some comments: "Just so you know, Frank, our contact with you will mostly be by phone. There will be no flowery conversation, just specific information regarding when and where the operation will take place. There should be no reason for you to have any questions, but if you do, ask them quickly and be specific." At this point, Joe chimed in: "You will be contacted each time by an unlisted phone number, so there will be no name associated with the number. We will open our conversation with 'all good?', and if there are no problems with you accepting the call, you will answer: 'A-OK'. Do you understand?"

"I got it. If you don't hear the 'A-OK', the call should come at another time. I am assuming that this is not a one-shot deal. May I ask how often or how many times I will get the call?"

Joe answered: "You'll get the call for as many times as we see fit. You could get a call two days in a row or not hear from us for a month. That will be our decision. Now, if there is nothing else on your mind, we have to get back to work."

The two men rose from their chairs and nodded to Tony. They turned to Frank and said that they would be "in touch." As they turned to go, Sal's suit jacket opened slightly revealing what Frank thought was a police detective badge. He blinked to get a clearer focus, but the opportunity had passed, and the two men were on their way out of the back room.

Tony and Frank were now alone in the room. Tony looked at Frank and started barking out orders, conditions and guidelines: "Frank, one of the first things you have to find is a warehouse that can store a large assortment of items. I don't care if you have to pay a small amount for the rental, but the warehouse has to be off the beaten path, if you know what I mean. Secondly, you know a lot of fringe guys who are just looking to be a part of an operation. Pick three of these individuals and be very careful with your choices. How these guys work and operate could account for your success or, unfortunately, your failure. You will be solely responsible for their actions, so think twice before accepting anyone. Thirdly and lastly, you have to acquire some hardware. You and these other individuals will have to be armed each time an event takes place. I can possibly help with a resource in that area. You and I will have one more meeting before the operation begins. Think about what I've said, and if you have any specific questions, hold them until our next meeting which will come shortly."

Frank understood all of the instructions that Tony laid out; however, he was concerned with the fact that there would be three other armed individuals with him. In Frank's mind, this just added to the significance of the operation which he was leading. He wanted to ask about the detective shield that he thought he saw, but, following Tony's instructions, he would hold that question for the next meeting.

Frank smiled and nodded his understanding to Tony. As he rose from his chair to leave, Tony called out to him one more time: "Frank, this is a big opportunity for you. With your success, you can bring a lot of money into the family, and you will earn the respect of the boss. However, if things go bad, the responsibility is going to be yours and yours alone. You will have to accept whatever praise or punishment comes your way. I will be in touch."

Frank left with his head spinning. However, this is what he wanted. He would make sure it worked out because if it didn't, Frank knew that, not only would he ruin his chances at moving up, but the fall from grace could be deadly.

Chapter Nine

The Sixteenth Birthday

It was a brutal nine months for both Marjorie and Jack. Marjorie was totally uncomfortable and irritable, while Jack was beleaguered working two jobs and catering whenever he could to the whims of his wife. However, although it seemed like it would never end, the day did arrive when Anthony, named after his grandfather, opened his eyes to the world outside of the womb.

The entire family was overjoyed with the new arrival, and Jack couldn't be happier having a son. Of course, after the birth, Marjorie could do very little, so everyone in the family helped her cope with the responsibilities of parenting. It took quite a while before Marjorie was able to handle everything on her own. It did seem, however, that she was in no hurry to take on all of the duties that came with taking care of an infant.

When the newborn family member was presented to Antonio, he took his namesake in his arms and said something to the effect that sounded like "hello Sonny." From that point on, Marjorie and Jack's child was known as "Sonny." Although formally he was "Anthony," the name "Sonny" was to stay with him for his entire life, and there was no push- back from anyone in the family.

Jack thought that the arrival of a new addition would bring him and his wife closer, but to his dismay and disappointment, it seemed to push them farther apart. Marjorie's total concern was for her son, and she acted like Jack didn't even exist. Jack was an understanding guy, so he gave Marjorie space with the hope that as time went on, she would warm up to him. However, that was not to be the case. Although it didn't get any better, it didn't get any worse. It stayed at the status quo which was not at all a desirable relationship in which the couple operated.

Because of the financial demands of supporting a growing family, Jack spent long hours working his two jobs. The monies from the bank account that Jack had started to offset the predicted increase in expenses quickly evaporated as Marjorie was now privy to the account's existence. She purchased much more than was needed to take care of Sonny. In fact, in Jack's opinion, she was reckless with her spending. The more Jack worked and brought home additional money; the more Marjorie spent.

Jack was beside himself, and he knew that he was going to have to directly address the problem and put his wife on notice that she had to be more prudent with their funds. He also knew that once he broached the subject with his wife, it would be the beginning of a war and an attitude that could last for weeks or even months. Marjorie was not very practical or understanding, and Jack hadn't realized how self-centered and selfish she really was.

Jack Martin had to plan the approach to his wife because he didn't want to make things worse between them. It was not like him, but he procrastinated for months before he built up the nerve and formulated a plan to address the situation. He decided that he would leave work early one day and surprise her with flowers and her favorite box of chocolates which he hoped would pave the way for an easy transition into discussing the financial problems facing them. This was a guy who faced fierce opponents in the ring but was actually frightened at what could result from a face-off with his wife.

Jack's plan, in addition to the flowers and chocolates, involved his coming home early to surprise his wife and actually help her with whatever tasks needed completion. So, he did just that. He left work early and picked up the surprise gifts that he was going to give to his wife. The more he thought about it, the more he felt that Marjorie would be amenable, especially after seeing the gifts, to reducing the amount of spending that was taking place. He almost felt good about his plan.

Jack arrived home in the middle of the afternoon when Sonny usually was napping. This was in his plan, and it was good because it would give him and his wife uninterrupted time to discuss the situation at hand. As he unlocked the front door and entered, he heard Marjorie speaking in the bedroom. He heard Marjorie mention her best friend's name, Dorothy, and realized that his wife was apparently on the phone with her friend. Jack did not want to interrupt Marjorie. She was very emphatic that she didn't want to be interrupted when she was speaking, whether it be in person or on the phone. So, Jack did not want to start out on the wrong foot, and he remained silent and waited in the kitchen for Marjorie to end her call. This step proved to be a move that would frame the rest of his time with Marjorie.

"Dorothy, I can't tell you how each day with him borders on disgust. I hate each day, and I can't bear being close to him. I've told you before that the only reason I married him was to get out of my house and out from under the thumb of my father. The only good thing that has come from this marriage is my son. Even though I would want more children, I couldn't bear giving myself to him again. Without my son, however, I would go crazy. What I have done is to accept the worst of the two evils, my father and/or my husband. Make no mistake, Dorothy, I suffer with the only decision I had to free myself from my father's rule."

There was silence in the bedroom which indicated to Jack, who couldn't believe what he was hearing, that Dorothy was responding to Marjorie's comments. His wife was quiet for quite a while listening to her friend. Jack stayed perfectly still, not wanting to alert his wife to his presence. With his fisted hands clenched tightly, his stomach turned as he realized that he was just an excuse for Marjorie's escape. She was very close to his family, especially Alice, and he wondered if Marjorie had ever confided in his sister regarding the feelings she had or didn't have for him. If that were the case, it would be an additional knife through his heart.

Jack continued to remain as quiet as he could when he heard Marjorie bid "good-bye" to her friend. Marjorie hung up the phone and exited the bedroom to see her husband, Jack, sitting at the kitchen table.

"Well, hello, Jack. What are you doing here and how long have you been here?"

"Marjorie, I've been here long enough to understand how you feel. It seems that I've been blinded by my feelings and have been made the fool."

"Okay, so you know how I feel, and why I did what I did. We are still married, and I guess we have to make the best of it for the sake of our son. We should still try to make things work out."

"Marjorie, understand what I am about to say. I will stay as part of this family until my son reaches the age of sixteen. When he reaches that age, I will leave you and Sonny. I will continue to interact with Sonny, but I will have nothing to do with you. As far as I am concerned, you are a necessary evil to me. From this point on, I will control all of the monies coming into this house, and I will make all of the decisions that have to be made. If you can't stand this arrangement or me, then, by all means, you can leave. My son and I will make things work out. Maybe, your father will take you back!"

Marjorie was taken aback by Jack's uncharacteristic attitude. She was shocked by his dictum which didn't leave much to choose from. Just as she was going to respond to Jack's comments, he rose from the table and grabbed the gifts that he was going to give to his wife and crushed them as he threw them into the garbage. He looked at Marjorie with disdain and emphasized his previous statement: "From now until Sonny's sixteenth birthday, we are two people who just happen to be living in the same house. Nothing more. As far as I am concerned, you are, unfortunately, the mother of my son, and I can't change that. However, you will be treated accordingly. Marjorie, sixteen!"

Jack left the house and was angry, shocked, and hurt. He had been strong in his response to what he had heard from Marjorie, but he now had to formulate a working plan as to how this co-existence would work. While this problem was thrashing about in his stream of consciousness, he had to find out if Marjorie's close ally, his sister, Alice, knew anything about this situation that was a total surprise to him. If Alice knew and had kept this from him, there would be hell to pay, and the family would see a side of Jack Martin that they've never seen before and would not want to ever see again!

Chapter Ten

An Irreversible Mistake

When Jack left the house, Marjorie immediately got on the phone with her ally in the family, Alice. She told Alice everything that happened and warned her that Jack was on the warpath. Marjorie had confided in Alice, so Jack's young sister knew all about Marjorie's feelings and the reason why she married Jack. Of course, Alice wasn't privy to all the facts and information prior to the wedding, but over time she had become an ally of Marjorie's and knew just about everything.

It was no secret to Jack or anyone else in the family that Alice and Marjorie were very close. In fact, Alice was the Godmother to Anthony for his baptism. Alice did not have a romantic partner, nor did she have any children who she had to care for or to whom she would have to direct her attention.

Because of those reasons and the fact that Alice was a bit of a rebel, she was a natural to become a confidant for Marjorie. Alice tried to calm Marjorie, thanked her for the call and told her that she would handle Jack. Truth be said, Alice did not know how she was going to deal with the fact that Jack knew Marjorie was only in their relationship to escape a situation with her father. Alice did feel, however, that Jack would approach her because of the obvious relationship she enjoyed with her friend, his wife. However, she, at least, had time to think about how she would answer Jack's anticipated accusations.

Antonio's family was widespread now. Only one of his daughters remained in the house with him. Although Mary had a fiancé, she opted to stay with her father and take care of him and the house. Antonio had aged relatively well, but still needed continuous attention. Mary was the one in the family who had the most patience with him, so it was natural for her to center her life around her father. Also, there was a good possibility that if anything ever happened to Antonio, the house would probably be willed to her. She was patient but also intelligent enough to know that having a house that was mortgage free would be an asset that very few would have. She would be able to save money and get those things in life that others would not be able to afford because of household expenses. Her fiancé was also on board with the arrangement and accepted the fact that when and if they married, he and Mary would be living in the one-time family residence. Excluding Alice, Mary was the only sibling not yet married. However, her wedding date was not too far off in the future.

After leaving Marjorie, Jack wandered around aimlessly rehashing what had just occurred. He was certain that he had made the right decision regarding his leaving as Sonny grew and reached his sixteenth birthday. But what was bothering him as much as the revelation that he heard was the fact that his sister, Alice, might have known the circumstances for a very long time. This concern drove him to head to Alice's shop. Without further delay, he wanted to find out what Alice knew, if anything.

It only took Jack about thirty minutes to get to Alice's work location. It was still early enough in the afternoon that Alice would still be at work. He approached the receptionist and explained who he was. In order not to give Alice time to prepare, he told the receptionist that he wanted to surprise his sister. The young woman was receptive to the idea of a family surprise, so the receptionist directed him to Alice's office. Looking through the glass window on the office door, Jack saw that Alice was alone. It was the perfect time to surprise his sister. He thanked the receptionist and entered the office. To say the least, Alice was totally shocked and probably a little frightened.

"Jack. You surprised me. What are you doing here?"

"Well, Alice, knowing how close you are to Marjorie, I am sure that by this time, you already know what went on this afternoon between me and her. So, let's get down to the nitty-gritty. Did you know about the real reason why Marjorie married me?"

Alice hesitated and that was confirmation to Jack that Alice knew something. In a raised and frustrated voice, Jack voiced his comments again before Alice had a chance to respond: "Alice, you're hesitating, and that would indicate that you have to think about what to say. I will ask you again if you knew the reason why Marjorie married me."

"Jack, calm down. I know that just like many other people who get married, she wondered if she had done the right thing. You know she lived under the tyrannical rule of her father, and she thought that maybe she jumped into another situation too quickly."

In almost a shout, Jack asked again: "Did she tell you that she married me just to get out of her father's house, and that she never really loved me? As a matter of fact, I hear that my mere presence disgusts her. Alice, don't beat around the bush. I am your brother, and you owe me the truth!"

"You're right, Jack. You are my brother, and I do owe you the truth. So let me tell you this. There were indications that Marjorie was not happy with her decision to marry you, but she never said to me that the only reason she married you was to get out of her house. I really don't think that is the case."

Jack yelled so loud that some of the workers came to Alice's office door. She put her hand up to indicate that everything was okay and motioned to them to get back to their positions. Jack stopped his comments and looked at Alice with disappointment and disdain.

"Alice you are a liar. You knew it for a very long time, and you kept it from me. I will never forgive you for that. Don't ever ask me for anything because, as far as I am concerned, you just happened to be someone that I know. A real sister would not have betrayed her brother. It's funny that you mentioned that there were indications that she was not happy. I don't remember your letting me know that you knew about her sad state of affairs. No, you kept that and the fact that you knew why she married me a secret. I despise you and also pity you for not having the good judgement and loyalty that you should have. You are worse than she!"

Jack turned away from his sister. He opened the office door and left it wide so that Alice could see his back for the whole time that he exited. Jack had mixed emotions as he left. He felt good getting certain things off his chest, but he was disappointed in his sister. It was hard to believe that Alice would favor a friend over her blood brother. If the situation were reversed, he would have never chosen someone else over his sister. Now, he had no use for her. He decided to have minimal contact with her and decided that, if asked, he would let the rest of the family know why his attitude toward Alice had changed.

Meanwhile, Marjorie knew that she blew the whole thing. She had never seen Jack so angry, hurt and demonstrative. At one point, she felt as though Jack might physically take his anger out on her, but to her relief, he didn't even threaten it. Marjorie was counting on Alice to smooth the waters as much as possible, but she was going to have to live with the fact that her husband knew exactly how she felt. That was surely going to be a major problem for co-habitation. She didn't know how he was going to act, and she didn't know how she had to act.

As soon as Jack left Alice's office, his pager beeped. When he looked at the screen, it indicated that his brother, Frank, was calling. He didn't feel like rehashing everything with him, so he initially decided not to answer. However, Jack felt that it was much too soon for Frank to know that he had visited his sister's office. Furthermore, it would be totally out of character for Alice to call Frank and whine to him. All things considered, Jack decided to find a public phone and call his brother: "Hey Frank, what's up?"

"What do you mean 'what's up'? I just got a call from Alice who was very upset and crying to me over the phone. With all of the crying, I really couldn't understand what she was talking about. What is going on, Jack?"

"You know what, Frank. I really don't feel like going through the whole thing with you right now. Let it suffice to say that the deceitful bitch that I married confided in Alice, and she decided that she was going to favor Marjorie over me. Although I felt like smashing her for what she did, I held back because she is my sister, but I have no use for her from here on in. When we have some time, and I cool down a bit, we can meet, and I'll explain the whole thing to you. For now,

I need some time to think about what to do in the near future. I need to be alone and clear my head."

"Jack, was it so bad that you have to take such drastic measures?"

"Frank, let's just say that if it was you, there would have been a number of beatings doled out. That's how bad it is. Don't judge me, Frank, and it's best if you stay out of it. I'll talk to you soon."

"Jack, don't forget who you're talking to."

"I never forget, Frank. That's why I'm telling you to stay out of it."

"Jack, that's not your decision. I'm already involved in it, and I want to talk to you."

"Well, Frank, I learned a long time ago that you don't always get what you want. However, in your case, I forgot that if you don't get what you want, you make sure no one else gets it either. Frank, stay out of it!"

With that, Jack hung up.

Chapter Eleven

Turn the Other Cheek

Jack was in no better mood after speaking with his brother. He decided to go over to his father's house where he was sure that he would find some of his sisters. It was now after work hours, and as usual, there was always one or two of the family members stopping by to see their father or just to visit with Mary. Jack wanted to set the record straight with everyone in the family before he was deluged with a thousand questions as to why he made such a "terrible" decision.

Jack was right. When he got to Antonio's house, he found his father, three of his sisters, and his younger brother, Michael. It was the usual setting for what had become the meeting place for the family, and as Jack entered the living room, he knew that the news had beaten him to the house. Everyone, including his father, stayed silent and stared at Jack as if he had just landed his spaceship on the front lawn. Jack looked around and was surprised that Marjorie wasn't sitting there with her best friend, Dorothy, and of course her family confidant, Alice. He nodded a "hello" to everyone and started his sarcastic silence breaker: "Well, I am so glad that everyone could make the party, and I am sure that, by now, you all have made your decision as to how I have overreacted, and how I have taken the situation to the extreme. I also know that you have my best interests at heart, especially since I am your brother, and you would only want the best for me. But before you pound me with questions that really have no relevance, let me explain what has happened because your source might be somewhat inaccurate and slanted."

Mary interrupted and spoke up before Jack could continue: "Jack, we know what happened. It is a difficult pill to swallow, but a decision like the one you've chosen affects the whole family. Can't we all discuss it and maybe come up with a better solution?"

"Mary, do you hear yourself? You want me to reconsider the fact that Marjorie has been living a lie and has led me down a path that, at one point, would definitely prove to be disastrous. The only difference between that scenario and the present one is that I beat her to the punch. I, not she, now dictate the rules of the game, and I guess that is difficult for all of you to accept. I would ask you all to put yourselves in my shoes, and then ask yourself what you would do. Do you really know the entire story?"

There was silence in the room. No one answered Jack's direct question. With this silence as a foundation, Jack decided to start from the beginning: "Well, since no one answered, let me tell you exactly what happened, not a tall tale from Alice, who was most assuredly influenced by a deceitful fraud, but by me, who still remains a pawn in a scheme that benefitted only one person, Marjorie."

Jack went on to explain, blow by blow, why he came home early from work, and how he hoped that his efforts might pump new life into their floundering relationship. He explained further how he heard his wife speaking to her best friend, and how she explained to her friend that she only married him to get out of her house. He emphasized the fact that Marjorie was heard to say that she was disgusted whenever he came near her. He told this small but influential family group that he was staying only until Sonny's sixteenth birthday because he owed that to his son. It had nothing to do with Marjorie or any attempt at saving what was dead in his eyes. He abruptly stopped speaking and looked at each person with a "well, what have you got to say, now?" stare.

Once again, and before he could go on to tell them that he had a strong suspicion that Alice knew what was going on for a long time and failed to let him know anything, Jack observed shocked faces and a deafening silence in the room. The silence was shattered, however, when the front door briskly opened to the appearance of the youngest female sibling, Alice. When she saw Jack, she stopped in her tracks and wondered if she should turn around and leave or stay and face the music.

Jack, feeling her indecision, faced Alice and said: "Just in time and just as expected. Since you're here, why don't you explain how you let a total stranger take advantage of your brother and continue playing him for a fool!"

Although old and weak, Antonio had heard enough. He got up from the chair, raised his hand in a "stop" motion and began to speak in a voice that was a mere notch above a whisper: "That's enough. I didn't raise any of you to act this way. Dominic (sometimes Antonio, for emphasis's sake, reverted back to his son's baptismal name), Alice is your sister, and you must respect her. Also, what you are doing is breaking up a family because of something that can be discussed and fixed. You have a son who needs a father and a mother. I do not want to hear any more of this disagreement. We are a family, and we have to act like one with respect and harmony."

The rest of the family was relieved that Antonio stepped in to quell the growing antagonism. Especially appreciative was Alice who foresaw more grief coming her way. Antonio, the father figure in an Italian family, was well-respected and somewhat feared. However, Jack was so incensed with the whole situation and his family's reaction to it that Antonio's comments did not put out the fire of rage that burned inside of him.

So, the oldest son in the family could not hold back his angst and spoke directly to his father: "Dad, you are asking me to respect someone who had no respect for me. She could have helped me in the very beginning, and maybe I wouldn't have been so receptive to having a child right away. Understand that I love my son, and I will do everything possible to make certain that he is comfortable and grows into a man of whom we can all be proud. But dad, with all due respect, if you were so deceived and betrayed, I am certain that your actions would be far more serious than my own. So, I ask you to understand that I cannot forgive and forget. My son will have a father and mother, but unfortunately, I have lost a sister."

All else had seemed to fail, so it was a natural consequence for the peacemaker in the family, Michael, to give it a try. He almost felt obliged to intercede. In a very calm but instructive voice, he asked that everyone take a step back and put themselves in the situation in which Jack found himself. Michael emphasized to the group that their brother had been betrayed, not once, but twice.

"Although I would be remiss if I didn't say that the ideal thing for Jack to do would be to turn the other cheek, I don't know if I could practice what I preach in such a situation. Sure, we all want to see peace in the family, but peace comes when we consider the feelings of others. None of us here are considering not only the anger that Jack is feeling but the debilitating hurt that comes with it. The family isn't the victim, his wife is not the victim, his sister is not the victim, and for that matter neither is his son. Dominic, or Jack if you prefer, is the only victim. We should be unified in helping our brother cope with the devastating information that he happened upon. I do not know if any of us here could handle the circumstances as well as Jack. I know that I couldn't."

Following his comments to the group, Michael addressed his next statement directly to Jack: "Jack, what can I do, no what can we do to help you?"

"Well, let me say this, Michael. You have definitely chosen the right vocation. I don't know if the pope himself could have attacked the problem as well as you have. Thank you for that. What I really need is for the family to understand that I want my relationship with my son, Sonny, to remain a strong and loving one. You all can help me do that by reinforcing the fact that I love him, and that my leaving has nothing to do with him. Also, I know that Marjorie has won a warm place in your hearts, and in some instances, a very warm place; however, I am asking that you remember that the same warm feeling that she ignites in all of you turned into a blowtorch against me. Just remember that I am your brother, and she is the one who hurt and deceived your brother. She may remain a friend to some of you, but she is nothing more to me than the mother of my son. And Michael, you are correct. Ideally, one should turn the other cheek, but unfortunately, in this case, I can only turn one way!"

Just as Jack finished his comments, the front door burst open, and a very angry Frank entered. He heard Jack's final comments about turning the other cheek and he addressed Jack: "We all have problems turning the other cheek, Jack, so I am going to help you." Frank approached Jack, clenched his right hand into a fist and landed it directly on the left side of Jack's face, forcing him to turn his cheek to the right. Jack was totally surprised by the punch and fell to the ground, hitting his head on the wooden floor. Jack was out cold. Frank looked down at his unconscious brother, and then looked at Michael and said: "See, Michael. It's not so hard to turn the other cheek!"

Chapter Twelve

Trust Me

After Frank's crude example of turning the other cheek, he abruptly left Antonio's home for a scheduled meeting with Tony Delfiato. This was a meeting to make sure that Frank had covered all bases and was ready to go. Frank had wasted no time in getting all the elements that he needed for the upcoming operation. The most difficult of these needs was the recruiting of three individuals who could be trusted and who showed some indication that they could use common sense.

Frank had to be very careful with his choices since these additional individuals were going to be armed. The last thing that Frank needed was a mishap involving the shooting of another person. So, he was very careful with his interviews as the words of Tony Delfiato repeated in his head: "You will be totally responsible for the actions of the individuals you chose. They can either add to your success or influence your failure!" There was no way that Frank was going to allow anyone to get in the way of his success. So, at this meeting he was going to reassure Tony that everything was set, and that he was ready for whatever came his way. Unfortunately, he could not know all those things that would come his way, nor the solution to the problems that would ultimately pop up.

Once again, he arrived early at the meeting location where he observed the two individuals who had attended the previous meeting heading for the building. He had assumed that today's meeting was only between himself and Mr. Delfiato. Apparently, he was wrong, as Sal and Joe entered the storefront location. Once he saw the two men arrive, Frank quickly exited his car and approached the building. When he entered the back room, Tony and the two other individuals were still exchanging "hellos" and small talk. That ceased once Frank appeared in the room. Tony Delfiato motioned to the three of them that he wanted to get down to the business at hand. So, without hesitation, Frank and the other two sat at the table to start the meeting.

Tony Delfiato asked Frank what progress he made with obtaining those items that were needed for the operation. Frank was glad that Tony started the meeting by calling on him because he was more than prepared to show everyone that he was capable of heading up the operation: "Just to bring everyone up to date, I have secured a large warehouse in the Bushwick section of Brooklyn. It is on a dead-end street and in an area that is not busy or frequented by many. Also, I have concluded my interviews with associates wanting to be part of this family's operation, and I believe that I have picked a good group of men."

Tony interrupted Frank after his last statement and commented: "Frank, what do you mean that you 'believe' that you've picked a good group? You had better know for sure that these men are good. As I mentioned before, if they fuck up, you are fucked. You do understand that, don't you?"

Frank was taken aback by Tony's interruption, but he recovered quickly: "Just a poor choice of words, Mr. Delfiato. I am very confident that they will add to the success of the operation."

"Glad to hear that, Frank."

Joe was the next person to comment: "Frank, you say that you have secured the warehouse. What does 'secured' mean? Are we paying for it? Did you make a private arrangement to get it? Is the owner now an additional partner in our operation? How did we get the warehouse?"

"Joe, I have known this individual for a very long time. I would trust him with my life. I will take care of him from whatever profit that I see."

Joe responded: "Frank, I hope you realize that you may very well be trusting him with your life."

Frank just nodded and smiled as Sal entered the conversation: "Frank we need to know more about the warehouse. How large is the warehouse? Are there any windows? How is the warehouse secured? Are there any cameras or an alarm system that we should know about? What about the lighting system and who will have access to the building? Lastly, will the warehouse be able to easily accommodate an eighteen-wheeler?"

This last question that was posed to Frank by Sal was the first real indication about what the operation entailed. Frank assumed that they would be storing goods in the warehouse, but now he understood that the warehouse would hold items that were being transported by truck. He still wasn't sure how the goods and the eighteen-wheeler were getting to the warehouse, but he was about to find out.

Frank began answering the questions in the order in which they were asked, and it seemed that the people present were pleased with the responses. There were some additional questions, and Frank easily had an answer for those too. It looked like the operation was a "go." However, just before Tony Delfiato was about to call the meeting to a close, Frank interjected with a question that had been floating in the air the whole time.

"Mr. Delfiato, you mentioned that you might be able to help me attain some hardware that I might need for the operation. Is that still the case or should I start looking for myself?"

"No, Frank. I have already spoken to my source and the weapons will be ready for you when you need them. I will let you know where and when to pick them up."

"Thank you, sir. I have just one more question. I am assuming that me and my group will be involved in hijacking trailer trucks. I do not have a problem with that, of course, and I imagine that I will be getting information about the individual routes and trucks from the two gentlemen sitting here. However, when we stop the truck, what happens to the driver, and who do we have available to drive the hijacked truck to the warehouse?"

Tony Delfiato responded: "Frank, you and your team will be wearing masks so there is no risk that any of you will be identified. When you stop the trailer, you will take the driver out of the truck, knock him out, and leave him on the side of the road and out of sight. When it is safe, a call will be placed to the police so that the driver can be found."

Frank interrupted: "Mr. Delfiato, none of my people have been trained in driving an eighteen-wheeler. How will we get it to the warehouse?"

"That has already been taken care of, Frank." Tony Delfiato pointed to a door at the rear of the room. Sal got up from his chair and went to the door to open it.

Tony continued to speak as a figure entered the room through the door: "Frank, I don't think I have to introduce you to your driver." The figure came out of the shadows and Frank immediately recognized him.

"Hello, Frank. It will be good working with you. You know that the church congregation doesn't pay much these days, so I had to find a gig that would help support me and my family. My early days of commercial driving allowed me to maintain a trailer license, but more than that, I have no problem handling the big rigs."

Frank sat there just staring in shock. His younger brother, Michael, who advocated for religion and all things that are good, was standing in front of him as the driver who would get the hijacked trailers to the warehouse.

"Michael, what are you doing? This is not for you. I don't want you involved in any of this. Leave now, while you still can."

Tony cut Frank off: "Hold on a minute, Frank. You are not giving the orders here. Michael wants a part of the action, and I have no problem including him. If you have a problem with that, maybe you should consider your involvement in this project. Michael comes with the same references that you do. He is Antonio's son, and that makes him a good prospect for inclusion. Michael will be the fourth person accompanying you to the scene. When all is done with the driver and the actual stop, Michael will drive the trailer to the warehouse. To allay some of your fears, he will not be involved in the initial stop, nor will he be approaching the driver. Also, he will not be carrying any weapons. He is just there to deliver the trailer."

"Mr. Delfiato, you know whether he is actually there when we take down the truck or not, he is just as guilty as the rest of us by association and conspiracy. He is too young to get involved in this. Isn't there anyone else who can do it?"

"There probably is, Frank, but I've made my decision, and it will stand."

Michael saw an opening and commented: "Frank, don't worry about me. I will be fine. You just take care of what you have to do and leave the rest to me."

Frank was shocked by Michael's attitude. He couldn't understand how Michael was okay with what was going down, but at this point, there was nothing that could be done about it.

"Okay, Michael, but keep your head down and don't take any chances."

"Thanks, Frank, but you have to realize that I am a deacon in the church, and I've got God on my side. Remember, 'In God We Trust'."

Frank just looked at his brother and shook his head: "Yeah, and you remember that God is the only one that you can trust. Don't turn your back on anyone."

The rest of the individuals did not take Frank's comments lightly, and they asked Frank what he meant by the statement. But his response was even more cutting than his original statement: "Two people at this table have already taken an oath swearing to God that they would uphold certain obligations, and you are asking me to explain what I meant by my statement. If you take a look in the mirror, I believe my statement speaks for itself."

Frank got up and turned to leave the room when he heard Tony Delfiato say that the meeting was not over. Frank looked at Tony and said: "We're talking about trust, aren't we? We need not discuss anything else, so **trust** me, the meeting is over." Frank headed for the door and left.

Everyone in the room was shocked, but no more than Frank himself! Tony Delfiato wasn't the only one with surprises!

Michael immediately tried to calm the waters, and he told Tony Delfiato that Frank was just concerned about his younger brother's safety. He further explained that Frank would be fine, and the operation would go off without a hitch. Apparently, Tony favored Michael and told him that he understood. He acknowledged that nobody likes surprises, and it seemed that Frank was totally taken by surprise: "I guess we all have different reactions when we are caught with our pants down. I am sure that Frank will come to his senses and reach out to me. It's good that you can stand up for your brother. I like that, and welcome to the family."

Chapter Thirteen

Don't Count on Blood

Michael left the meeting in search of his brother, Frank. Although Tony Delfiato said that he understood, he implied that he was owed an apology. So, Michael was going to make sure that Frank did the right thing. Michael knew the local gin mill where Frank usually hung out, so he headed for that bar. It was located in Brooklyn, not far from where Frank and he grew up. The problem was not finding Frank in the bar, but explaining to him why he never told his brother that he was involved in the operation. Michael knew that if he told Frank in advance that he was going to work for the mob that his brother would do everything to stop it from occurring. That is the main reason why Michael never told his brother anything. However, Michael didn't know if that reason was going to satisfy Frank who not only was surprised but embarrassed by the revelation.

While Frank and Michael were involved with mob concerns, Jack was in his father's house recovering from the cold-cock punch that Frank had landed. Jack had been out cold for at least thirty seconds before his siblings were able to bring him back, and that was the only time, including his entire boxing career, that he had been knocked out. In addition to the impact of the punch, Jack had hit his head on the tile floor. So, the damage was twofold. He was groggy and hurt, both physically and emotionally. He was also embarrassed that a one time, very decent, boxer could be laid out with one punch.

With the attention of everyone directed at the results of the argument between the two brothers, the immediate concerns over the matrimonial problems plaguing Jack's situation fell to the rear. However, the dilemma still existed for everyone there, and especially for Jack. But Jack knew what he had to do, and he had made his decision which was ironclad.

As Jack slowly regained his balance and wits, he began to hear the expected warnings from the rest of the family. Those warnings consisted of persuading Jack to let the incident roll off his back because everyone knew how angry and nasty Frank could get. The group was afraid that if Jack decided to even the score and pursue Frank that the oldest brother in the family could be severely hurt. In a fit of rage, no one put it past Frank to use whatever he could, including a gun, to immobilize a threat. So, one after the other, they all tried to persuade Jack to "just let it go."

Jack was keenly aware of Frank's temperament and his overall attitude in wanting to be on top all of the time. Jack was also aware that Frank might regret his actions afterward, but at the time, he would use anything and everything to come out the victor. Jack was smart enough not to presently provoke a reoccurrence of today's events, but there would be a time when Jack would have the opportunity to even the playing field. He would just bide his time.

Jack was able to allay the fears of the rest of the family by telling them he understood how impulsive Frank was and that sometimes, his brother could not control his anxiety. And at those times, Frank just lashed out. Jack explained to them that what everyone witnessed was Frank's anxiety influencing his actions. After Jack's long explanation of what had occurred, Antonio and the rest of the family were relieved that there would not be any follow-up on the part of the oldest brother. Jack was more than convincing in his overall tone and attitude, but he was reeling inside.

Michael's instincts were correct, and he found his brother in the neighborhood bar. There were only a few other patrons in the bar, and Michael was happy about that. When he approached his brother, Michael did so very slowly and carefully, apologizing as he got closer. If looks could kill, Michael would have been dead. Frank turned to his brother and growled at him: "What the hell do you think you are doing? It's bad enough that you're getting involved in mob life, which I do not agree with, but you did it in a way that not only demeaned my reputation and standing, but implied that I have no control over my own family. Also, tell me. Does Antonio know that his youngest son is now involved with the mob? I am sure he isn't aware of your participation. If he did know or had any inkling, he would have already called me to the house telling me to make sure that I derailed any attempt by you to become mob tied."

Michael didn't interrupt Frank's diatribe. He knew that Frank had to get a lot off his chest before he would listen to anything. So, he waited patiently and finally saw the opportunity to speak: "Firstly, Frank, I apologize if I embarrassed you or slighted you in front of Tony Delfiato and the other two men. I hope you know that it was never my intention to do that. I didn't realize that my showing up at the meeting would, in any way, negatively affect you. I will make sure that I right the ship and correct any mistakes that I've made. To answer your question about Dad, no, he doesn't know anything about my involvement. I know what his reaction would be, and I knew what yours would be. That's the reason why neither of you knew. Understand Frank, I need money, and the way that Mr. Delfiato has set up the operation, there is very little risk in it for me."

Frank raised his hand and told Michael to stop: "You don't understand what is going on. Just because you are not involved in the actual "taking of the truck" doesn't mean that you aren't equally guilty of the high jacking. If things go south, you are just as guilty as the rest of us. I do not need my younger brother facing the possibility of jail time. If you need money, let me know, and I will back you for whatever you need."

"No Frank. I am not going to depend on you for what I need. I have to make my own way in life, just like you. This is an opportunity where I can make good money with very little risk. Also, I am sure that we will all share in the goods that come our way. So, besides saving money, I will be able to get things without having to buy them. It's a win-win situation for me. One last thing, Frank. You walked out on Tony Delfiato, and although he acknowledged that he understood why you reacted the way you did, reading between the lines, he is expecting an apology from you so he can save face in front of everyone who was present."

"What? After what he did, he expects me to apologize to him. He must be on drugs. I reacted the same way he would have reacted if the tables were turned. There is no way that I apologize to that blowhard!"

"Okay, Frank, you got it off your chest. You know how the hierarchy works. He's the boss, and there are certain things that you don't do to the boss. One of them is to never embarrass him. Frank, you did that. Let's be grateful that he accepts your apology and let's both continue to work for him."

"Well, listen to my little brother telling me the ways of the mob. Unfortunately, you're right. For me to remain a part of the operation, I will have to go back to him with my tail between my legs and beg for his forgiveness. I can do that or just kill him!"

"Frank, don't even joke about that. You never know who is listening. Saying something like that could get us both killed. I'm not ready for that!"

"Take it easy, Michael. I will do the right thing and get everything straightened out. I will call Tony and ask if I can speak with him. I will apologize to him one-on-one, and then, I will repeat my apology when we all meet again. That should take care of Mr. Delfiato's feelings, and it will allow him to save face."

"I think that is the way to go, Frank. It will get us both off the hook. I am really looking forward to working with you, Frank. We should make a ton of money. Thanks for understanding."

"Michael, I'm still not happy with your working for organized crime, and I feel lousy deceiving our father. However, it seems that there is very little that I can do about that now, but remember, little brother, I am heading up the operation, and I will determine what has to be done, and when it is to be done. You know that there are weapons involved, so stay out of the way until I say that it is okay for you to come forward. Do you understand?"

"Yes, Frank, I totally understand. I will wait for your orders before I do anything. You are the on-the-scene boss, and I won't forget it."

"I hope that's not sarcasm, Michael. Even though you are my brother, I'll cut your legs out from under you if I have to. Do not make the mistake that blood will give you special privilege. If anything, it makes you more vulnerable to inspection and observation. Also, understand that it was your choice to come on board, and I will have no hesitation in spilling blood, if I have to."

"You won't have to do that, Frank, for two reasons: I'll not do anything to incur your wrath, and secondly, I will never give you the chance to spill any blood."

Frank understood his brother's comments, but he might have misunderstood Michael's possible intent. He now dwelled on the old adage that warned: "beware of the enemy within." Did he now have to worry about his younger brother's enthusiasm and obsession with making additional money? He decided to play everything very close to the vest. He would have liked to think of Michael as an expected ally who would have his back, but he had this uneasy feeling that to let his guard down, even with his brother, could result in a situation where his position and success would be challenged. Little brother or not, that wasn't going to happen!

Chapter Fourteen

Whatever You Have to Do

Marjorie felt the need to meet with her ally, Alice, so she called her and asked for a time when they could meet. After what had occurred in the house with her brother, Alice was a little reluctant to push the envelope. However, she gave into Marjorie's pleas and decided to meet with her after work. Alice knew that if Jack found out that Alice was meeting secretly with Marjorie, there would be no coming back from his disgust and disappointment.

When they finally met, Marjorie continuously mentioned to Alice how scared she was that Jack would do something to hurt her or Sonny. She was convinced that Jack was going to get back at her for deceiving him. No matter what Alice said, she could not convince her friend that Jack would never stoop so low as to inflict physical pain on her, and especially not on their son. She repeated to Marjorie over and over again that no matter what she thought of her brother, he was not heavy-handed. However, it became apparent that all Marjorie was looking for was sympathy for her uncomfortable position. As Alice realized this, she discontinued her discourse about Jack's potential actions and went on to ask how Marjorie was going to handle living in the same house with the person about whom she told her friend, Dorothy, that she was disgusted when he came near.

Marjorie got the hint and went on to other subjects and concerns. She knew that she no longer had access to the bank accounts and her credit cards, which were under Jack's name. They had been destroyed. She was at the mercy of Jack's mandates and living conditions. It was going to be difficult for her, and she was looking for whatever help she could get from Alice. However, Alice was not her only "go-to" person. Marjorie was well liked by the other females in the family also. It wasn't just going to be her alone against Jack. In fact, she was sure that she would win over some of the other females. It would take time, but she would succeed.

Jack recovered from the incident in his father's house and also from the devastating turn of events to which he had been privy. He continued to be the father that his son needed but also directed much of his time to bettering his position in the garment industry. Although he was disappointed and somewhat disgusted with his sister, Alice, he felt terrible that their relationship had deteriorated. She had always been an ally of his, and he felt very protective of her. She was the youngest, and he was the oldest. That natural positioning brought them together in a bond that maybe the others didn't share. It was this bond that caused such a hurt when Jack found out that Alice had kept significant secrets from him. He could not forgive her actions, but he didn't want to remain in such a strained relationship with her. He decided to call her and tell her that he wanted to meet with her.

Just as Jack decided to make a phone call to his sister, Alice, his ever-present pager activated and his sister, Mary's, number appeared on the screen. It was unusual for Mary to be contacting him, and he became concerned that something might have happened to his father. He quickly contacted her and got right to the point: "Hello, Mary. Is everything all right? Is dad okay?"

"Hi Jack. Yes, everything is fine, and dad is okay. However, I paged you for him because he said that he would like to see you as soon as you are available. He seemed very serious when he asked me to contact you. Jack, do you know what could be on his mind? Is everything okay between you and him? You know at his age we don't want to worry him about anything."

"Mary, I was going to ask you if you knew why he wanted to speak to me. Apparently, you don't. And you don't have to remind me about dad's age. I know very well not to worry him or give him any reason to be concerned. I would guess that he is still bothered by what went on in the house between me and Frank. Don't worry, I'll ease any concerns that he might have. I will leave work a little early and come straight to the house. See you in a bit."

Jack left work and headed to see Antonio. He didn't like his father to worry, and he was always concerned about his father's health. Even though he left early, there were delays, and what was usually a thirty-minute trip turned into a good sixty minutes. Jack was tired and frustrated when he arrived at the house. Mary was waiting and probably looking out of the window for his arrival because as soon as he approached the front door, she was there holding it open.

"Hello, Mary. I would have been here sooner, but, as usual, there were delays. How are you doing?"

"I am doing fine, Jack. But dad is patiently waiting to speak to you. He seems a little on edge."

Jack walked into the house and found his dad sitting in his favorite chair just staring into space.

"Hi, dad. How are you doing? I understand that you want to speak to me about something."

"Hello, Jack. I am glad that you could come over. I want to talk to you about something that is very important."

Antonio looked over to Mary, who had been standing a short distance away. He waved his hand in a dismissive manner to tell Mary that what he had to say was for Jack's ears only. Mary was annoyed that she could not be privy to the conversation, but there was no way that she was going to second guess her father's decision. She nodded and left quietly for the other room.

As soon as she left, Antonio, in whispered tones to make certain that no one else, especially Mary, could hear what he was about to say, started speaking: "Jack, you are the oldest of my sons. And although Frank has taken over, I need to rely on you to do something for me."

"Sure, dad. What do you need?"

"I need you to get Michael out of the claws of the crime family."

"Dad, what are you talking about? Michael isn't involved in any crime family. You know that he spends his time assisting with church events. Heck, he is even a deacon in the church."

"Jack, although I am not physically connected to the family anymore, I still have many friends there. I got a message that Michael is involved with Frank doing the work of organized crime. I know that Frank is a lost cause, but I need you to get Michael out before it's too late. Do that for me, Jack."

"Dad, are you sure that whoever told you could be trusted."

"Son, I would trust him with my life."

"Okay, dad. I will get right on it, but you know it is going to be difficult if Frank has given his 'okay.' I guess I will start with Frank, although I don't know how much cooperation I will get from him. I am sure he doesn't want to hear from me, and because of his sucker punch, he is going to be on guard regarding anything I have to say. But I will try my best, dad."

"Jack, I am an old man, and I don't want to die knowing that I allowed my youngest son to go down a path that could only end in disaster. I was able to stop you, and now I am asking you to stop him. And Jack, do whatever you have to do to get Michael out. Whatever you have to do!"

Jack had never seen his father so serious or determined. And Jack was going to fulfill his father's request. Frank or no Frank, Jack was going to do what he had to do!

Chapter Fifteen

Jack Needs Help

On the way out of his father's house, Jack stopped at the door to the kitchen where Mary had secreted herself in an effort to hear what was taking place. Jack told her that it was just a little problem that he would handle, and that it was nothing to worry about. She seemed to accept Jack's comments and thanked him for coming over so quickly. Jack said "good-bye" to both Mary and Antonio, and headed to where he believed he might find his brother, Frank.

Jack was also familiar with the neighborhood bar where Frank stopped to unwind and have some friendly conversation with the bartender who had been there forever. Although he always consumed a good amount of alcohol, Frank never let himself get to the point where he was oblivious to what was happening around him. In other words, he was never dead drunk. There was too much riding on his ability to lead and manage, and, for a number of reasons, he couldn't afford to have his reputation damaged. So, although his visits to the bar allowed him to mellow out, he never lost his mental acumen, and was always ready to do business. Also, in the particular line of work in which he was involved, one's personal safety and security depended, many times, on his ability to respond to whatever came his way.

So it was on the day that Jack arrived at the bar. The inside of the gin mill was dimly lit, so Frank did not immediately recognize his brother. When he did, Jack was surprised by how Frank welcomed and greeted him. It was as if nothing had ever happened between them. This took Jack by surprise, and it forced him to rethink his approach to Frank and the problem at hand.

"Hey, Frank. I'm glad I caught you. I want to discuss something that seems to be bothering dad."

Before Jack could go on with the conversation, Frank raised his hand and said: "Let me guess. Dad found out that Michael is working with me and the mob. I knew it couldn't be kept a secret for any length of time. Dad has too many connections who are still associated with the organization. So, you are here, Jack, to get my cooperation in helping you get Michael out of the situation that he is in. First of all, I don't know if I can do that, and secondly, I really don't think that our young brother wants to sever his connection to the mob and Tony Delfiato."

Jack responded: "You don't seem to understand, Frank. At this point, it's not what Michael wants that counts, it's what dad, you and I want that counts. You know that Michael is much too young to get involved in this type of garbage. He has a bright future ahead of him, and this can only ruin that. Frank, I need your help. Dad needs your help, and most of all, and he probably doesn't even realize it, Michael needs your help."

"Understand, Jack. I didn't bring Michael into this. As a matter of fact, I was shocked when he appeared at a meeting with Tony Delfiato and others. It was at Tony's invitation that Michael came to the meeting. So, he bypassed me and dealt directly with Michael. I wasn't included in any of it. Because of that personal touch that Tony employed, it is going to be even more difficult to get Michael out of the agreement he personally made with the boss. You know how those things work. You don't go back on a contract that you made with anyone in the family. Michael agreed to come on board, and it is going to take more than my influence to break an agreement. Do you have any suggestions? You're not that far removed from what goes on behind closed doors. Or even better, did dad have any words of advice?"

"No, Frank. He just wants me to stop Michael anyway that I can. I am not sure if I know a way, but I am willing to try anything to stop Michael before it's too late."

"Jack, you're missing my point. It is probably too late already. What do you want me to do? Do you want me to just go up to Tony and tell him that Michael is out, or would you want me to tell him that Michael made a mistake, and our family wants him to bow out? Do You realize how ridiculous that sounds? Tell me, Jack. I will ask you again. What do you want me to do?"

"Frank, maybe you could talk to Michael, and then he could go to Tony."

"I've already had a conversation with Michael. There is no way that either one of us is going to convince him to leave."

Jack was out of suggestions. He sat down next to Frank and ordered a drink. All he could see was his father's face, almost begging him to stop Michael's involvement. Jack also understood where Frank was coming from. In addition to the fact that Tony Delfiato would be pissed at Michael for breaking an agreement, Frank would also suffer the negative ramifications that were sure to come. After all, Michael is Frank's younger brother, and this would only show Tony Delfiato that Frank couldn't even control a younger sibling. How was he going to control the group of thugs that he put together to successfully manipulate a hijacking operation? Jack felt like he hit a brick wall. He didn't want to give up and disappoint his father, but it seemed like he was all out of options.

As Jack drank, his mind began working overtime. A new idea filtered through the maze of negatives. He turned to Frank and said: "Suppose we work on Michael through divine influence." Frank was clueless and looked at Jack with a "what the heck are you talking about?" face. Jack continued:

"There is nothing closer to Michael than the church. Maybe, I can get the pastor to speak to Michael and convince him that he's making a bad decision."

Frank, displaying an air of disbelief, answered: "Let me get this straight, Jack. You are going to tell the pastor of Michael's church that you need his help in getting your brother out of an agreement that he made with a boss in organized crime. You are going to ask him to speak to Michael to tell him that he should not be dealing with the mob. Hey Jack, maybe you could convince the pastor to attend one of Tony Delfiato's meetings and persuade all of them to correct the error of their ways. Jack, If I didn't know better, I'd say you were on drugs."

"Yeah, I guess I'm grabbing at straws, but I have to come up with something or dad will be devastated. Could you at least think about it, and maybe something will come to mind?"

"I'll think about it, Jack, but whatever it is that could get Michael out of this is going to be a reflection on me. So, although I'll give it some thought, I will do it half-heartedly."

"That's typical you, Frank. You always only think of yourself. It is so important to dad that he said he didn't want to die knowing that his youngest son was part of the mob. That's how deep this is, and that's how badly dad wants Michael out of that family. I don't think that dad's death is imminent, but you never know. And once Michael starts with the mob, you know there is no getting out. Dad knows that all too well."

"Okay, okay. I will try to come up with something where Michael has an escape route and where I and Tony can save face. I can't promise anything, but I will try."

"Thanks, Frank. Let's toast to your success in finding a way out for Michael."

They touched glasses and ordered another drink. However, it was getting late, and they both had other things that they had to do. So, Jack got up from the bar stool and told his brother that he had to leave and that hopefully they would be in touch. But before Jack could leave, Frank grabbed his arm and said: "By the way, how are things going at home? I know it's got to be rough staying there when you know how she feels, but for Sonny's sake, I think you are doing the right thing. I know that he is kind of young to actually realize that things aren't the way they should be, so if you need any help with anything, just let me know. Speaking of kids, Colleen and I apparently can't have any naturally, so we are thinking about adopting. As you know, she is crazy about kids, and it's the only way that we can have a family."

"Frank, that was a mouthful. Yeah, it's rough staying there, but I said I would, and I will. Sonny seems to be fine, and you're right in that he is much too young to know what is going on. But come the time when he can understand, I will tell him everything. He deserves to know the truth. Lastly, it's great that you are willing to adopt. I don't know if I could do that, but I am sure Colleen is happy with your decision. Well, I guess that's enough for now. I have to go."

They shook hands and Jack turned to go. Frank turned to the bar. Jack stopped suddenly and came back to where Frank was sitting. Jack tapped him on the shoulder, and when Frank turned around, he was met with a huge right hand across his chin. Jack didn't want to kill him, so the punch was only at three-quarter strength. Frank was knocked off the bar stool and landed on the floor laying on his back. Jack reached down and partially pulled Frank up by his shirt collar: "Don't ever raise your hands to me again. The next time it could be fatal for you."

Jack dropped his brother back down to the floor and walked out with a satisfying smile on his face.

Chapter Sixteen

Apologies and Contracts

Although things were not very good with Jack, Marjorie ingratiated herself with the rest of the family as much as she could. She was well-liked but she needed as much support as possible. For reasons that were far from obvious, the family looked at Marjorie as having been the injured party. The female siblings were unanimously in support of trying to persuade their brother, Jack, to reconsider his stance. Marjorie was very convincing, and she had a lot of experience in deception. Her greatest ally, Alice, who didn't learn by her past mistake, led the charge to soften Jack's approach and ultimatum. Alice spent a lot of time working with Marjorie, and their bond grew even stronger. If one didn't know better, a person would surely assume that the blood relationship was between Marjorie and Alice rather than between Alice and Jack.

Jack was not oblivious to what was going on in his family. He saw what was happening, and he realized how persuasive Marjorie could be. Jack not only saw the family's prejudice against him, but he felt it. He understood that no matter what he did or said he wasn't going to influence their opinion. So, he didn't try. He directed his focus on his son and his work. In addition to those two main directives, he now was charged with finding a way to get his youngest brother out of the clutches of organized crime. His father was depending on Jack's ability to succeed. Although he left his brother, Frank, in a compromising position on the floor of the local bar, he hoped that his brother understood that if the tables had been were reversed, he would have done the same thing. In fact, living in a sphere of violence, physical persuasion, and organized crime, Frank might have thought that Jack's action was indeed praiseworthy. That was the way of the world in Frank's closed society.

Jack was excelling in responsibilities and monetary rewards at work. He was the foreman in the new shop, "Allure Lingerie", and the company was growing. As the foreman, Jack was charged with many productive aspects of the total operation. He was also responsible for contracting other companies for materials and resources that were needed for the final product. One of those potential companies was owned by his sister, Alice. Although Jack was aware of this situation, Alice was even more alert to the possibility of a lucrative contract with "Allure."

The Garment Industry is a rather close-knit association. So, when something breaks in the industry, all companies are aware of the news. When Alice found out that "Allure Lingerie" had succeeded in landing two very large production contracts, she realized that her brother, Jack, would have a significant role in hiring resource companies to supplement the needs of "Allure" as it proceeded to comply with the dictates of the contracts. Alice's company was one of those companies that could be considered as an eligible material resource outlet.

The situation threw a monkey wrench into her goal to persuade Jack to think differently on the home front with Marjorie. She valued Marjorie's friendship, and she wanted to help as much as possible, but in practice, Alice valued the almighty dollar and power to a much greater extent. So, Alice decided to swallow some humble pie and mend fences with Jack. She did this, not for her own personal relationship, but for a potential advantage in the procuring of a production contract.

Alice decided to visit Jack at his shop. It was a huge gamble, but it was the only way that she could convince Jack that she was sincere in her effort to apologize, an apology that she hoped would lead to Jack's agreement to include her company as one of the resource shops. A contract, the size of which was the largest that she had ever been privy to, was at stake. And she had a potential advantage since her brother was the one who was examining proposals and who would be influential in the final decision.

As soon as Alice found out about the open bid for contracts, she headed for Jack's shop. She decided not to call ahead because it would be more difficult for Jack to refuse a meeting with her if she were there in person. Jack was no fool, and he would know that she was only there to apologize so that she could speak to him about getting a contract. So, she really had to be convincing in her "mea culpa." She could pull it off; she had to.

It took just about thirty minutes for Alice to arrive at Jack's shop. During that time, she developed a strategy that she hoped would pull on Jack's heartstrings and his loyalty to family. She even rubbed her eyes to indicate that she had been crying about the whole situation. It wasn't about her relationship with Jack; it wasn't about her loyalty to family; and it wasn't about making things right. It was about Alice and her potential success in the business and production world – her female positive attack on the garment industry.

When she entered the building that housed "Allure Lingerie," she was greeted by a receptionist who inquired about her reason for being there. Alice mentioned that she had to speak with her brother, but that she didn't want to be announced. The receptionist thought it to be an unusual request, but she wasn't going to deny Jack Martin's sister in any way. The receptionist showed Alice the way to her boss's office, and then left Alice to do what she wanted. Alice knocked on the door and entered. To her chagrin, Jack was not in the office. Apparently, he was out on the production floor with his workers. This was going to make it more difficult for Alice to carry out her charade. However, she was determined to carry out her plan, and she started looking around for her brother. The shop was rather large, so it took a little while for her to locate Jack. When she saw him, she stayed out of sight until he finished speaking with a worker.

When Jack finished with the instructions that he was giving to one of the garment cutters, he turned to head back to his office. It was then that Alice stepped out of the shadows and became obviously visible to her brother. When Jack looked up and recognized his sister, he stopped and just stared. He began shaking his head in a negative manner and didn't move. Alice was taken aback by Jack's actions. She was at a loss as to her next move. This wasn't the way it should have gone. She had to think on her feet and get Jack to speak with her in private. Alice was quite manipulative and not new to unexpected challenges. She clutched her hands together in front of her and mouthed her apology: "I am so sorry."

Again, Jack just shook his head, but this time he started walking toward her. When he got close enough, he said: "Alice, why are you here? As if I didn't know."

"Please Jack, just give me a chance to explain. I don't want us to continue on the way we are. I've always looked up to you for guidance and advice. I don't want that to end. I know that I should have told you as soon as I knew something was bothering Marjorie. I was wrong, and nothing like that will ever happen again."

Jack motioned to Alice and said: "Let's get off the floor and go into my office. I don't need the rest of the shop to know how dysfunctional our family has become." She complied, and they headed for his office. Alice felt a little relieved that Jack invited her into his office. It showed that Jack, at least, wanted to listen to what she had to say. She would only have one chance to convince her brother that she was sincere, and that sincerity would be the influencing factor in her achieving the goal of landing a resource contract.

Jack entered his office and moved behind his desk to sit down. Alice was relegated to the visitor's chair with the desk acting as the business buffer. This wasn't a good sign, and Alice knew it. Before Alice had a chance to continue her practiced apology, Jack spoke up: "Alice, I know that you do not think me the fool. Your half-hearted apology comes on the heels of the news that we are looking to contract with certain companies to assist us in completing the mandates of the contracts that we have just signed. You can't deny it, so let me here your pitch."

"Jack, do I need a pitch? I am your sister, and you know how a resource contract will help my company. In all sincerity, I do realize how you felt when you found out that I knew and didn't tell you about Marjorie. However, I thought that I could convince her to reconsider her feelings and give the two of you a chance. Apparently, I was wrong on two fronts: one, I couldn't convince her because her feelings were too strong on the negative side, and two, I should have realized that there was little or no chance that you would let the situation slide off your back. Yes, Jack, I want to land a contract, but understand that I do realize that I was wrong."

"However, Alice, you only realized that you were wrong and that you needed to apologize when you heard about our contracts. Wow! What a coincidence. Can you deny that?"

"No, but just consider your contracts as a catalyst for my apology. And I thought that what Frank did was totally wrong and that you deserve to set things straight. He never should have hit you or put his hands on you. That was wrong, and he needs to know it."

"Alice, let me allay your fears. I will give your bid attention, and if I see that you will be able to help us with the contracts, I will consider recommending it. On the situation with Frank, I am surprised that you haven't heard that I got my day in court with our brother. He also came face to face with the floor."

She was shocked, but before Alice could say anything at all, the office door swung open, and Frank filled the doorway.

Chapter Seventeen

A Father's Message

Both Jack and Alice were shocked and surprised to see their brother, Frank, standing in the doorway. With this unexpected arrival, both Jack and Alice were at a loss to understand why Frank was there. Jack was concerned that Frank wanted to get back at him for knocking him to the ground in the bar. Alice just felt that she was in the wrong place at the wrong time.

Following his surprise guest appearance, Frank addressed his startled siblings: "Well, I'm glad I finally caught up with the two of you. Alice, I went to your shop only to be told that you had gone; and Jack, I wasn't sure that you would be working in your shop today knowing that you were meeting with a number of people regarding the new contracts that were splashed all over the industry newspaper. However, fate was kind, and I found both of you."

It was Jack's shop and his office, so he was the first one to speak to his brother: "Okay, Frank. So, you found both of us. What do you want? I am sure you're not here to shoot the bull."

"Hold on, Jack. This may benefit both of us. You wanted me to give some thought to Michael and his predicament. Well, I have, and I think the answer is standing right next to you. Yeah, our sister, Alice. You and I know that Michael has a soft spot in his heart for Alice since she is the youngest. He is closest to her than any of us. We should work on Michael through Alice."

Alice was confused. She heard her name being bandied about, but she had no idea what Frank was talking about: "Hey, wait a minute. First of all, what are you talking about? And secondly, how do you know that I want to do anything with, for, or about Michael? Why don't you let me in on the plan before you decide that I am the right one to complete it?"

Now, Jack took the lead and explained to Alice all about his visit with their father, and how he pleaded with Jack to stop Michael from becoming an active member of the mob. Alice was taken aback when she heard that Michael was involved with Frank and the crime family. She expressed her shock and concern: "I can't believe that Michael would even think about working with the mob. He is the last person in the world that I would expect to align himself with a crime family. For goodness' sake, he is a deacon in the church. Do you really think that he would get involved with the mob?" This last question was directed at both Frank and Jack. However, the fact that they both just stared at her and said nothing, answered her question. She continued: "Well, what do you think I can do? He is a grown man. Do you really think that I can persuade him to do or not to do anything? I think that you both are overestimating the influence I may have over him."

Jack answered Alice's question: "Whether we are overestimating or not, Frank is right. At this point, you are our best option. We have no other alternative. For our father's sake, and also to protect Michael from going down a path that will probably only result in pain and disappointment, we need you to try."

Alice retorted: "Michael is no fool. He is going to know that one or both of you have asked me to speak to him. How else would I even know that he was involved with the mob? Okay, I will speak to him, but I wouldn't expect any drastic change in his decision. I would have thought that you, Frank, would have greater influence over what he was doing than I. When he came to you, why didn't you just tell him 'No'?"

"Alice, you're assuming that he came to me. I was just as surprised as you are now that he was involved with the crime family. He showed up at one of the meetings at the invitation of one of the bosses. I had no control over whether he got involved or not. That's why we find ourselves in the present situation. We are trying to abide by our father's wishes, but I really don't know if we can change anything. Alice, you are our last resort."

Alice said nothing but just started pacing around the office. After what seemed like an eternity, she finally turned to both of her brothers and said that she would arrange a meeting with Michael and try to convince him that he should reconsider what he was doing. She then turned to Jack and put him on the spot: "Jack, whether I succeed or not, I am sure that my company will be one of those awarded a resource contract with "Allure Lingerie." That's correct, right Jack?"

"Alice, you should be doing this because you want to help your brother, Michael, and it's the right thing to do. It shouldn't be done for what you can get out of it. However, I know how materialistic you are, so, yes, I'm sure that your company will be awarded one of the resource contracts."

Alice was happy with Jack's response. She didn't have to do anything but speak to Michael. That was a walk in the park, as far as she was concerned. She didn't even have to succeed. Her visit to Jack had worked out better than she had anticipated. Thank you, Michael!

Frank was satisfied with the outcome of this brief sibling meeting. He had nothing further to discuss regarding the situation. However, he did have something to say to Jack: "Jack, you should have never left the ring. You still have plenty of punch in those fists. I'll admit that I was surprised by your unexpected retort to my previous actions. However, even if I wasn't surprised, I would have still landed on the floor. Also, I applaud the fact that you wanted to balance the scales, but I wasn't happy with the implied threat that you ultimately levied. I am sure that you understand that the word 'fatal' may very well apply to you also. So, making threats like the one you made could come back to haunt you. But for now, I am willing to call it 'even'."

Alice had just learned that Jack had sought revenge and had exacted it. So, when Frank rambled on about Jack's retaliation, she was learning about what actually happened. Having experiences with both Frank and Jack, she didn't trust that Frank had called it "even." He had never accepted anything that was equal or even. What he wanted and usually got was the advantage of being ahead or on top. So, as she listened to Frank, she knew that the interaction between her brothers was far from over. But for now, she decided to say nothing and planned on a meeting with her brother, Michael.

As the informal meeting was coming to a close, and Frank and Alice started to leave Jack's office, his office phone began ringing. Jack called out to his secretary to find out who the caller was. The secretary responded that Jack's sister, Mary, was on the phone. It wasn't often that Mary called, and when she did, it was never good news.

"Hello, Mary. What's up?"

"Jack, I am at the hospital with dad. He has had a heart attack. It was a mild attack, but at his age, the doctors are monitoring him very carefully. He is asking for you. Can you come down to the hospital as soon as you can?"

"Mary, I will just clean up some things here, and I will head to the hospital right away. Is there anyone else with you?"

"No, Jack. Everyone else is working, but I called you first because he is asking for you. Please come quickly."

"Okay, okay. I am on my way."

When the phone rang, and Jack was told that it was Mary at the other end, he motioned to Frank and Alice to wait before they left. When Jack got off the phone with Mary, he told his siblings what Mary had relayed to him. They both offered to go with Jack to the hospital, but he emphasized that Antonio was asking for him. He told Frank and Alice that they were more than welcome to come with him, but that he needed some time alone with their father. He also explained that he was more than sure that their father was going to ask about the progress that Jack made, if any, with solving the problem involving Michael. Alice and Frank understood and told Jack that they would make sure that he had some time alone with their father. They left the shop and headed to the hospital.

They all had their own vehicles, so they proceeded in caravan style. It was the beginning of rush hour, so traffic was steadily building, and what should have been a twenty-five-minute ride resulted in a frustrating forty-five minutes. Jack was first to park his car and headed to the registration desk. He inquired about his father and was told the room number where Antonio had been taken. Frank and Alice were close behind and heard the room number, so they also headed that way.

When all three siblings arrived at the room, they saw Mary pacing outside in the hallway. She heard them coming and turned to them with a very solemn and concerned face. Mary collected herself and explained to the other three what was happening: "Dad apparently has had another heart attack. The emergency team is treating him now, but from what I've seen and heard, this attack was much more serious than the previous one. I hope dad has the strength to pull through. And I don't know, even if he survives, what condition he will be in as a result of the potential damage. I guess we just have to sit and wait."

Alice added: "And pray."

There was a lot of activity in Antonio's room, and his children saw resuscitation equipment quickly moved into the room. It could only be assumed that the doctors were having a tough time keeping Antonio alive. In a short time, the activity seemed to decrease, and the hospital door to Antonio's room opened. A doctor came out and approached the group. He showed regret and disappointment: "I am so sorry. We tried everything that we could, but his heart had been so weakened by the first attack that he could not recover from the second one. Again, I am very sorry. You may go into the room if you like."

The three siblings hugged one another as the tears began to flow, and they realized that the head of their family was gone, and an era had ended. They collected themselves and went into the room. Antonio seemed very peaceful as if he was sleeping, but they all knew how final this visit was. Jack and Frank said that they would notify the rest of the family, and Mary didn't argue with their decision.

When the time came for them to leave, Mary intentionally stayed a few steps behind. Frank was in front with Alice, and it gave Mary a chance to get Jack's attention. When she tapped him on the shoulder, he turned and before she could speak, he asked: "Did dad tell you what he wanted to speak to me about?"

"No, Jack. He just repeated that he wanted to speak to you. He might have had an inkling though that he might not be able to hold on until you arrived. Just before his fatal attack, he handed me this piece of paper and whispered that he wanted me to give it to you. He said it was only for you, and he folded it closed. He didn't want anyone to know about the message, and he definitely didn't want anyone to see it."

Although Mary was more than curious regarding the folded message, she dared not disobey her father's orders. Even though he was gone, his dominance remained, and Mary followed his orders to the letter.

Out of the sight of Frank and Alice, Mary handed the folded, sealed message to Jack. He placed it in his pants pocket until he was alone. When Jack finally split with his siblings, he took the sealed message out of his pocket and opened it.

Quickly reading it, all he could do was yell: "No! no! no!" Jack held onto the wall to stop himself from collapsing and falling to the floor. He started to uncontrollably sob which for Jack was a totally foreign emotion.

Chapter Eighteen

Unexpected Funeral Arrangements

Jack couldn't believe what he had read. Jack was the oldest child in the family, and the only one who could read and write in the Italian language. When he opened the paper and read the message he saw: *"Mi stanno uccidendo."* Automatically translating it into English, Jack saw: "They're killing me." Jack reread it and reread it. It didn't change. His father was telling him that his death was not natural but planned. Someone wanted his father dead. Why? For the life of him, he couldn't understand why anyone would want Antonio dead, nor who would plan such a heinous act. Jack had no reason to believe that his father wasn't on point. For the most part, Antonio had all of his faculties and very rarely exaggerated an idea. Jack felt that his father wouldn't have left the message if he wasn't sure of its content. Over a period of time, somebody planned Antonio's death. Jack would not rest until he found out who and why, but for now, he would not trust anyone with the information that his father had left him. Unfortunately, Jack strongly believed that if Antonio's message was true, the culprit had to be a family member or someone very close to the family.

Jack now looked at each family member as a possible suspect in his father's death. He decided to order an autopsy to see if a substance might have caused a heart attack. However, there was no rush to do that since he was the one who would ultimately make the funeral arrangements. Jack was going to get to the end of this mystery, and he felt sorry for the individual or individuals who had anything to do with his father's death. There would be no involvement with law enforcement; there would just be Jack Martin's justice.

Antonio had been taking a number of different medicines, any one of which, taken to the extreme, could have lethal consequences. It was common knowledge in the family that in addition to other ailments, including diabetes, Antonio had a weak heart. This made him vulnerable to heart attacks and heart failure. Too much of any of the medicines, including NSAIDS for severe headaches which he constantly experienced, could easily act as a catalyst for a fatal heart event. The entire family and even some people outside of the family knew of the conditions that Antonio had to endure. It would not be difficult for someone to intentionally increase the amount of medicine that Antonio took without his knowledge. But what perplexed Jack was why anyone would want to. He didn't know, but he would definitely find out.

Between work, figuring out how to get Michael out of the clutches of organized crime, and getting all of his father's belongings together, Jack had little time to get to the funeral home. However, the funeral director was a friend of the family and wasn't concerned with any delay. When Jack finally found the time to visit the director, he was going to tell him that he wanted an autopsy done. Jack wanted to know if the results would show any foreign substance in his father's body. If there was, then Jack might be able to connect the substance to a specific individual and discover a clue to the perpetrator.

After approximately three days, Jack cleared enough of his obligations to be able to speak to the funeral director. Following the initial salutations, Jack told the director exactly what he wanted. However, Jack did not understand why the director seemed so confused. His reaction forced Jack to inquire if there was a problem: "You look like you don't understand what I want or what I am saying. Is there a problem with doing the autopsy?"

"Yes Jack. There is a major problem with an autopsy since we have already cremated Antonio's body. We are holding his remains until the memorial service."

"What are you talking about. Who told you to cremate the body, and who is making arrangements for a memorial service? I wanted an autopsy."

"Jack, did your brother know that you wanted an autopsy done? He came to me and told me that the family had decided on cremation, and that he was interested in a memorial service. I did what he wanted."

"My brother? Which brother came in to see you?"

"Your brother, Frank, said that he was handling everything. Understand, Jack, I had no reason to doubt him. So, I cremated the body and was waiting for him to let me know when he wanted the memorial service. I am sorry if there was a misunderstanding, but Frank didn't leave any room for doubt."

Jack was livid. No one had contacted him, and the responsibility for taking care of the funeral arrangements was definitely his. He left the funeral home and told the director that he would be in touch with him. He also emphasized to the director, who seemed very disturbed over what had occurred, that the fault was not his, and that he would straighten things out with his brother.

When Jack got out into the street, he couldn't get to a payphone quick enough. He dialed Frank's home number, but unfortunately, there was no answer. Jack only left a brief message that told Frank that they had to meet as soon as possible regarding Antonio's funeral arrangements. Jack tried, as best as possible, to maintain a calm tone over the phone. He didn't want Frank to automatically go on the defensive, but Jack was really curious why Frank jumped at the opportunity to have their father's body cremated. Many things were going through Jack's head, but the primary point that kept bombarding his stream of consciousness was that Frank wanted the body cremated so that there was no evidence, and no one could prove that he was involved in the murder of his father. Of course, it was a stretch because Jack couldn't fathom that a son of Antonio would plot to kill him, but the thought kept rebounding in Jack's mind.

Jack kept his father's message in his pocket as he headed for the local bar where he hoped he would find his brother, Frank. Once again, fate was kind. Not only did he find Frank at the bar, but surprisingly, he also saw his sister, Mary, sitting next to Frank. He thought it odd that Mary was there, but then he thought that maybe she was taking their father's death badly, and her brother Frank was there to console her.

"Well, hello you guys." Both Frank and Mary were shocked to see Jack. Since neither one had seen Jack enter, they were surprised when he spoke up.

"I figured that I might catch Frank at the bar, but I'm rather surprised to see you here, Mary."

She responded: "Yeah, this not a place that I usual frequent, but I was feeling down, and Frank offered to buy me a drink so, we came here. There is so much to discuss."

"You're right about that, Mary. Frank, what possessed you to go to the funeral home and take charge of funeral arrangements for dad? You knew that it was my responsibility to do that. Why did you step in, and why in the world did you have dad's body cremated?"

"Hey Jack. I knew you were involved with so many other things that I thought I would give you a break and handle the funeral arrangements. Why should you have to shoulder all of the responsibility? I thought that I was doing a good thing. Before you ask further, I had him cremated so that we wouldn't have to have a long line of mob figures coming to pay their respects at a wake. We don't need that kind of notoriety. So, we will have a brief memorial service, and his former associates can send their regrets to the house."

"Frank, don't you think that you should have conferred with the rest of us before you made such a dramatic decision. You know that the final decision should have been mine, and you took that away from me. I don't appreciate that no matter why you say you did it. Is there anything else you decided on that I should know?"

Mary, who was usually very docile and who never really intervened when any of her brothers discussed family matters, decided to add her sentiments: "Jack, you almost sound like you're angry because Frank tried to help out. All he did was relieve you from some of the many responsibilities that you have. I think it was really nice and considerate of him to take some of the stress and burden off your shoulders. You should be thanking him not coming down on him."

Jack and Frank were both surprised by Mary's comments because she usually had nothing to say and just went along with the flow of things. So, when she added her comments, the two brothers just looked at her and then at each other as if to say: "Is that, Mary?"

When Jack finally recovered from the shock of Mary's participation, he turned to Frank and said: "Frank, Mary is right. I appreciate your taking the bull by the horns and making my life a little easier. Thank you, Frank, and thank you, Mary."

Jack put both his sister and brother at ease, but in the back of his mind he wondered why they were together in the bar. It was not in Frank's persona to console anyone at any time if it didn't benefit him. Also, Mary was never that close to Frank. In fact, at times she would ridicule his activities in organized crime and refer to him as a "wannabe." So, the whole situation did not sit well with Jack. The outrageous thought that Mary and Frank might have had something to do with their father's death circulated in his mind. If that were the case, and most likely it wasn't, whether they were family or not, they would pay. Jack would find out!

As he left the bar, Jack gently clutched the message from his father and mentally promised him that the message would burn in his heart until the truth was known. Jacked hoped, however, that the truth had not been right there in front of him and had just slapped him in the face.

Chapter Nineteen

Success and Risk

Alice kept her word and made arrangements to meet with her brother, Michael. She didn't think that she would have much success in convincing him of anything, but she was going to try. No sweat. However, if she didn't succeed, she was still going to get a resource contract from "Allure," and that's all that counted. Even though the main thing on her mind was the contract, she really didn't want to see Michael get involved, like Frank, in any mob activities. She also realized that it might be too late for him to bow out. One just didn't decide that he no longer wanted to be a part of that organization or a particular operation. Unfortunately, once you were in, it was quite difficult to get out.

Alice and Michael met at a local restaurant in Brooklyn, not far from where Mary lived. Alice was the first to arrive, and she picked a table that afforded privacy for the two of them. Michael arrived shortly after Alice was seated at the table. When he arrived, he had a smirk on his face. So, Alice asked him why: "Well, hello Michael. What's with the smirk? You look like the cat who swallowed the canary. Speak up. Tell me why you have that ridiculous grin on your face. Share it with me, so I can laugh too. It tells me that you know something that I don't. Is that right?"

"Well, they've run out of options, and I guess you are the last resort. Don't take that as an insult. You should consider yourself the last of the big guns."

"Michael, what the hell are you talking about? I just want to talk to you. We haven't seen each other for a while, and I want to catch up."

"Sis, I know you are trying your best to disarm me, but let me tell you from the get-go that I have no intention of discontinuing my association with Mr. Tony Delfiato or with Frank's operation. I have agreed to take part in it, and I'm going to do what I have to do. So, why don't we save a lot of time and talk about something else."

"You think you know it all, Michael. Unfortunately, this time you hit the nail on the head. You know that once you start with the mob, there is no getting out. I am not about to lecture you, but you know that you are risking your reputation, your freedom, and possibly your life. Aren't you too smart to do something like that?"

"Alice, I've weighed all the risks against the fact that I need money for my family, and my needs far outweigh any risks. I will only have a small part in any operation, and I will get paid well for my efforts. I know that probably Frank or Jack or both of them sent you to persuade me to reconsider, but first, it's too late to do that, and secondly, I don't want to ask out. It is an opportunity for me to get the things that my growing family needs. I am not going to look opportunity in the face and say 'No'."

"Okay, Michael. I've tried. But besides your brothers wanting you out, I also would feel a lot better if you stayed on the straight and narrow. If you need money, you can always come to me or anyone else in the family. You don't have to resort to the mob."

"Thanks, Alice, but I don't want to depend on anyone else. My family is my responsibility, and I have to deal with their needs. I appreciate your generosity and also the fact that you too really care about my welfare, but I have to handle this myself. I promise that I'll be careful not only for you but for my family too. I feel bad that I disappointed dad, but I'm sure that if he was in my shoes, he would be doing the same thing. In fact, Alice, he did do the same thing, and the family benefited by it. You, me, Jack, Frank, we all benefited from dad's associations. I just want a chance to better my life and my family's. I'll be fine."

As far as Alice was concerned, the conversation and her efforts were concluded. She nodded her head in understanding and ordered drinks for her and her brother.

The rest of their meeting was actually enjoyable, and it did serve to catch up on a lot of things regarding their family and the loss of their father. Antonio had treated both of them with kid gloves with Michael being the youngest male and Alice being the youngest female. They were the babies in the family, and they missed their dad's extra special attention. They finished their drinks, and they hugged each other as they left the restaurant. Michael, again, thanked her for her concern, and Alice pleaded with him to be careful. They smiled and went their separate ways.

Alice wasted no time in contacting Jack. She told him how the meeting went, and that there was no convincing Michael to abandon his plans with the mob. Although Jack was disappointed, Alice's report was no surprise. From what Frank had mentioned, Michael couldn't wait to start reaping the rewards associated with the operation. Jack called Frank and told him what Alice had said. Although Jack knew that, by her tone, the resource contract was uppermost in Alice's mind, he felt that she was also personally concerned about Michael's safety and well-being. Jack wasn't aware that her concern and his were going to be amplified that very evening. Frank had gotten a phone call.

The two men, Sal and Joe, who were at the meetings with Tony Delfiato, got information that they relayed to Frank. Sal made the call mentioning the code "All good," and Frank's response: "A-OK" was given. The information contained details regarding an eighteen-wheeler that would be in the area that same evening. It was carrying a vast variety of electronic devices which could easily be stored and ultimately sold to various buyers. The details were very specific since Sal and Joe were agents for the Federal Highway Administration, Department of Transportation. This was the epitome of the wolf in the hen house scenario. It was their responsibility to chart the truck routes and make certain that the journey would be a safe and secure one. These two corrupt agents had been involved in other illicit activities, but this operation was one in which a much larger profit could be realized. They knew what the trucks would be carrying and the specific routes that they would take for the delivery.

Following the phone call from the agents, Frank had to work quickly to notify his group that they were going into action immediately. Frank worked out the procedures that the group would follow, and he pinpointed the location that the agents said would be the best site for the stop. Frank arranged for the group to meet at approximately eight in the evening and then proceed to the location to meet the truck by nine. Frank had two different vehicles that would be employed for the stop. Everything was all set including the distribution of weapons that Frank hoped would never have to be used. He arranged for his brother, Michael, to ride with him. When the stop was made, and the driver immobilized, Michael would be the one to drive the trailer to the warehouse where it would be unloaded and secreted for a time.

The hijack group was at the location with plenty of time to spare. So far, everything looked good. There were almost no cars on this back road, and night had come, so it would be difficult for anyone to identify the hijacking team or their vehicles. The agents had been right on the money with their details. The truck approached at the approximate noted time. Forcing it to the side of the road went more smoothly than Frank had imagined. The hijack team was masked, and the driver offered very little resistance to the armed team. Frank made certain that the driver was tied up and placed on the side of the road and out of site of the trailer. At that point, Michael exited the vehicle that he was in and entered the cab of the trailer. He started the engine, and with the escort of his partners in crime, headed for the warehouse that Frank had secured.

The entire hijacking went extremely well, and the whole team was relieved that they hadn't encountered any obstacles to their activity. They all felt emboldened that this new operation was going to be a walk in the park, and one which paid outstanding dividends. It was easy money, and for Michael, money was his only goal. Michael's part in the operation was the least risky, and he actually enjoyed driving a trailer-truck again. It took just a little while for Michael to get that comfortable feeling he always had when he drove these rigs. He was feeling that way again. The warehouse was about forty minutes from where the group had stopped the trailer. There was no interference or problems on the way, and before long, Michael was backing the trailer into the warehouse. The warehouse doors closed, and the hijacking team, under the leadership of Frank Balaticco, celebrated their first success. It would be the first of many.

For Frank, this success and the ones to come in the future, could mean that there was a possibility for him to move up in the organization, especially now that his father was dead. Although Antonio was liked by many in the organization, he had made enemies with some who were in the higher echelons of the family. With Antonio gone, however, that friction and angst was gone too. Hopefully, with the success of his operation and the elimination of the stumbling point of his father's personality conflicts, the rails would be greased for his rise into a position of more responsibility and more rewards.

Michael was beside himself with the satisfaction of success and the benefits he was about to realize. However, he was blinded by those specific benefits and unable to see the obvious risks. Just because he didn't see them, however, didn't mean that they weren't there. In the future, he might very well get a close-up view of the risks that were surely hanging over every action that he might have to take.

Chapter Twenty

What She Heard

Time marched on, and there were many developments in the Balaticco family. Mary and her husband now owned the house that formally belonged to her parents, and she was pregnant with their third child. The number of children in the family saw a huge increase with every sibling, except Alice, having happily accepted the responsibilities of parenthood. Although Frank and Colleen could not have their own children, they did adopt, and they were raising a son of their own. The original Balaticco family was growing by leaps and bounds, and family get-togethers now resembled a crowd attending a country fair.

Marjorie and Jack had been tolerating each other for some years now, and that existence was in no way a rewarding one. They had been avoiding each other in everything except those things that pertained directly to the house or their son. However, Marjorie never lost her close connection to the family. She was still welcomed at family happenings and still maintained an extra close relationship with Alice. Much to Jack's disappointment, Alice and Marjorie had become what amounted to best friends. In fact, it seemed that the family treated Marjorie like the victim and not the offender. Although Jack was always more than welcome to interact with the family, it was Marjorie who commanded their attention. Maybe it was because of the fact that Sonny, who some in the family, like Alice, fawned over, was always with her when she visited. However, Jack did still maintain a close relationship with his son. Sonny didn't suffer from the strained relationship between his mother and father. In fact, he probably got more attention because of it. He definitely felt the increased warmth and attention that the family offered in their attempt to buffer any tension or divisiveness that his parents demonstrated. Sonny became the child of the family.

No one in the Balaticco family was financially suffering. With Frank and Michael having an increased cash flow, success was spread throughout the family. Many items that members of the family wouldn't ordinarily be able to afford were now part of their possessions. Many of the items were, of course, a direct result of the activities in which both Frank and Michael were involved. So, not only were Frank and Michael greatly benefitting from the illicit activities of the crime family, but their immediate family was also feeling the rewards of the hijacking operation.

Things were going so well for Frank that there was a very good possibility that he was going to move up in the crime family. He already had meetings with members of the hierarchy to discuss additional charges and responsibilities. As far as Frank was concerned, as long as nothing with the hijacking operation went wrong, and it continued to produce dollars for the family, he would be elevated. He had been leading the hijacking operation for a few years now with no obvious snafus. In fact, he was so confident in how well it was going that, at times, he just remained in one of the vehicles as the others did what they had to do. Michael was working out well, and if Frank was elevated, he decided, much to the anticipated opposition of Jack and Alice, that he was going to recommend his brother for a more significant position. He had discussed this with Michael, and his younger brother was straining at the bit for more responsibility, and therefore more money.

Jack still had the piece of paper that his father had given to Mary. Unfortunately, because of pressing obligations, Jack hadn't devoted the time that he should have regarding the investigation of his father's death. However, he often took his father's handwritten message out and stared at it. Although he wasn't any closer to finding out if, in fact, someone had killed his father, he made a list of those people who benefitted by Antonio's death. On top of that list were two of his siblings: Frank and Mary.

With Antonio gone, the hard feelings that some of the mob bosses had for the Balaticco family evaporated. This, more or less, cleared the way for Frank's potential rise in the crime family. And from what Jack had learned so far, there was a strong possibility that Frank was being considered for bigger and better things. In Mary's case, she now had sole ownership of the house where the family had resided. The house was mortgage free and in good shape. With the debt of an active mortgage gone, Mary, her husband, and their two children did not suffer from any financial burden.

So, in Jack's eyes, both Mary and Frank benefitted the most from Antonio's demise. It was tremendously difficult to believe that any one of his children would plot to expedite Antonio's death for personal gain. He had been a good father to all of them, and to assume that any one of them would stoop so low was against all that Jack believed. Too much time had passed, so Jack had to put his own personal beliefs aside and look at the information and clues that he might have before him.

Jack was very suspicious of the fact that Frank had taken it upon himself to have scheduled the funeral arrangements with a contract for a cremation. Jack also was suspect of the meetings that Mary and Frank had at the local bar. They had never met before, and they weren't even that close. Also, it was beyond Frank's stoic personality to be a consoler, something that Mary stated was the reason they occasionally shared drinks and time at the bar. He had no other leads or thoughts, so Jack decided to home in on the sibling connection. Was it possible that the two of them worked together to gain their individual advantages? He wouldn't put it past Frank, but he couldn't see Mary as a co-conspirator in their father's death. However, in his life, Jack had seen stranger things happen.

Alice had reaped her rewards, and she couldn't be happier. Things were going exceptionally well for her. In between ordering supplies, directing personnel and signing subcontracts, Alice made time to visit her sister, Mary. She had heard from Jack about the meetings that Mary had with Frank. Alice understood that Mary was still having difficulty dealing with their father's death after all this time, and so she decided to see if she could help Mary cope. They were not that far removed in age, and they had, at one time, socialized together. So, Alice had a special relationship with her sister, and she thought that she would surprise Mary with another visit, and see if she could lighten the load. Alice did not get along exceptionally well with Mary's husband, so she decided to visit Mary during the day when her husband was working.

Since Mary liked surprises, Alice didn't give her any warning that she was going to visit. Alice also got some pastries that she knew Mary liked. As far as Alice was concerned, it would be an afternoon of wine and pastries. She was looking forward to surprising and comforting her sister. Between traveling and stopping for goodies, it took Alice about an hour to reach her former home. She looked at the house differently now though. It was where her sister and her sister's family lived.

Alice approached the house very quietly and didn't ring the bell. Luckily, the front door was unlocked, and Alice was able to enter without notice. As Alice moved further into the house, she heard Mary speaking to someone. The sounds were coming from the kitchen, and this afforded Alice a greater advantage in surprising her sister. She remained quiet until she reached the archway that led to the kitchen. Alice still heard Mary speaking, and now realized that Mary was on the phone. Alice hid behind the arch and waited for Mary to terminate her conversation. It was impossible for Alice not to hear, at least, one side of the conversation, and she realized that her sister was talking to her brother, Frank. As certain parts of the conversation became clear to Alice, she couldn't believe what she was hearing. She heard statements like: "Are you sure, Frank, that the funeral director will never say anything? I worry that someone will ultimately find out. After all this time, I still can't sleep. I can't eat. I can't concentrate because I'm always thinking about the fact that we killed our father."

Alice held her breath. She just wanted to get out of the house without Mary ever knowing that she was there. She started backing up toward the front door and almost made her escape when she heard her sister: "Alice, what are you doing here, trying to sneak into the house?" Because of Alice's position, Mary had mistakenly thought that her sister was coming into the house rather than leaving.

"Hi, Mary. I was coming in to surprise you. I heard that you were still having a bit of a problem dealing with dad's death, so I decided to come over and surprise you with some pastries as long as you supplied the wine."

"That's so nice of you, Alice. I guess Jack or Frank mentioned that it was bothering me. I don't know if Frank mentioned it to you, but I even met with him a number of times just to have a drink and vent. It's really nice of you to come over."

"No problem, Mary. I totally understand. I feel the same way. I guess we both could use a little respite from the everyday disappointments and sorrows. Why don't we sit down and have some of your favorite pastries while we drink ourselves into oblivion?"

"That's a great idea, but I have to be sober when my kids get home."

"I get that, but we still have plenty of time to indulge. Oh, by the way, I spoke to Frank recently to find out how Michael was doing. Originally, I tried hard to persuade Michael to steer clear of the mob but look how well he's doing now."

"Yeah, the money is good, but I'm sure the risks are high."

"Have you spoken to Frank or Michael lately. I've sort of lost touch with them. I know that Jack is doing well, but like you, he thinks about dad's death a lot. I don't know exactly what it is, but there is something bothering him about that whole situation. Do you have any idea what it could be."

"No Alice. I haven't the faintest. I didn't realize that he too was still suffering from the loss."

Alice responded: "I'm sure he will figure it out whatever it is, but it is annoying that each time I see him, he asks questions regarding dad's time right before he died. Has he questioned you on anything?"

"No, not really. Although I don't see him that much either."

Alice got a last jab in: "Well, Jack is a smart guy. He'll figure it out."

By the look on Mary's face, Alice had succeeded in alarming Mary even more. If she did have something to do with Antonio's death, then Alice wanted her to fess up. By planting the seeds of concern and worry, Alice hoped that keeping such a secret would be too great a task. Alice wanted her sister to let the family know what she and Frank had done. It was not going to be Alice who would reveal such a betrayal and heinous act.

She knew that there would come a time when Jack would put two and two together and find out that Mary and Frank had contributed to Antonio's death. And when that time came, all hell would break loose. She had kept a secret from Jack once before and suffered from it. She wasn't sure if she should do it again. This time there would be no coming back as far as Jack would be concerned. She didn't want to lose him or his business. Alice was suddenly struck with the realization that again, she had to make a decision, one that could spell disaster and turmoil for the entire Balaticco family.

Chapter Twenty-One

No News is Good News

Alice left Mary that afternoon with a knot in her stomach. She was sickened to believe that her siblings had planned her father's death. She was so conflicted that she actually felt nauseous as she walked to her car. She got in the car and just sat there for a while thinking about the options that she might have. It also gave her time to sober up a little. Learning what Mary did, Alice drank more than she should have and now she was suffering from over imbibing.

She was afraid that once Jack knew that Mary and Frank had been involved in Antonio's death, that he would stop at nothing to seek justice for their actions. That justice could consist of many things including physical harm, jail time or even death. The more Alice thought about the situation, the sicker she got. It got to the point that she could no longer control her nausea. As quickly as she could, she opened the car door and deposited all that she had consumed that afternoon onto the street. She felt physically better after she vomited, but her problems and concerns still remained. She didn't have the luxury of putting off her decision. If she waited, Jack would be furious with her. If she let him know immediately, the turmoil would immediately begin. She kept asking herself why she decided to visit Mary at all. If she just would have called, she would not be in the predicament in which she found herself. Unfortunately, that was not the case.

Alice waited a while longer until she felt a little better. She drove to her home where she wanted to shower and collect her thoughts. One way or the other, she would have to make a decision afterward. If she decided to let Jack know what she had heard, she would not tell him via a phone call. She would ask to meet with him. Doing that would at least give her a chance to calm her brother. Although she knew that Jack would be livid once he found out that his brother and sister were involved in Antonio's death, she wanted the opportunity to at least try to persuade him to keep his head. It would be difficult, and she didn't want to be a catalyst for another act that could easily place Jack's freedom and safety in jeopardy.

Jack Martin was out with his son. They had gone shopping for some athletic equipment and now they were stopping at a local restaurant for dinner. Sonny was getting a lot older and not too far from his sixteenth birthday. Jack thought that it might be a good time to ease his way into explaining what had occurred between him and Marjorie, and to further explain to his son, Sonny, why his parents were going to separate.

Jack and his son enjoyed a good relationship, but Sonny was aware that things were not good between his parents. He saw no love or caring between the two, but merely a situation where it seemed like they just tolerated each other. Sonny was an intelligent kid, and he knew that sooner or later his parents would reach a point where they could no longer live together. So, when Jack started the conversation at dinner with: "Sonny, I think we have to discuss some things that are going to affect you, me and your mother," Sonny was somewhat prepared for the anticipated comments by his father.

"Son, I'm sure you realize that for any relationship to last there has to be feelings of love and caring. Unfortunately, I found out early in our relationship that those feelings did not exist for your mom. It was very difficult for me to accept that situation, and I told your mother, at the time, that I would only stay in the relationship until you reached the age of sixteen. I stayed in the relationship because I wanted to be close to you, and you deserved better than living with only one parent. But I hope you understand that I can't stay any longer than what I've stated. For all these years, I had to live with the realization that the woman I married only agreed to my proposal to escape the terrible situation in her own family.

She used me to implement that escape. I only found out accidentally one afternoon when your mother was speaking to her friend on the phone. But understand, although she has not been a good and truthful wife to me, she has been a good mother to you. You should hold no bad feelings for her. I am sorry, son, but there is no other way."

"Dad, I knew that there were problems between you and mom, but I didn't know that they were that bad. Do you really have to leave?"

Before Jack could answer Sonny's question, Jack's pager started beeping. Jack looked at his screen and saw Alice's number. It was not often that Alice would call, so he interrupted his conversation with his son and told him that he had to make a call. He utilized the restaurant's phone.

"Hello, Alice. What's up? Is everything okay?"

"Well, no, not really, Jack. It's important that I speak to you as soon as possible."

"Alice, unless it's an emergency, I am out to dinner with my son. Could it wait until tomorrow?"

"Yeah, it could wait, but I can't. It's bothering me, and I'm sick over it. The quicker we talk, the better it will be for me."

"Okay, Alice. When I finish with Sonny, I will give you a call, and we can meet. It won't be that late, but I have to stay with my son for a while. I'll call you as soon as I am through."

"Thanks, Jack. I'll be waiting. Please don't take too long. Good-bye."

Sonny realized that his father had just engaged in an important phone call, so he told his father that he didn't have to stay with him at the restaurant. He wanted to continue to talk to his dad, but Sonny saw how concerned his father seemed to be over the call. However, he also wanted a chance to try to persuade his dad to stick it out and stay with him and the family as long as he could. Sonny found it hard to believe that his mother would do such a thing to his father, but he knew that his dad had no reason to lie to him.

Jack answered Sonny: "No, son, I am not going to leave. I will have plenty of time later to take care of the phone call. You are more important, and your understanding of the situation is most important to me. I want you to know that no matter what, our relationship will not change. I will always be here for you, and you can depend on me whenever you need to."

"I know I can, dad. But you know it won't be the same once you're out of the house. If you can, could you think about trying to make it work out?"

"Sonny, I've tried for the past sixteen years. Things will not change between your mother and me. We remain civil with each other, but that's all there is. I really can't try anymore. We have both been living a life without love or concern. That's no way to live. As you get older, I am sure you will more readily understand. I will try my best to make certain that our relationship and your life doesn't change.

Although I will not physically be in the house, I will be close by."

"Dad, I am going to miss you, but I also want you to be happy. I also want mom to be happy. So, if separating gives you and mom a better chance to be happy, then I understand."

"Thank you, Sonny. You're an intelligent kid, and I have great hope for you. I appreciate your understanding. So, what do you feel like eating?"

Jack and his son stayed in the restaurant for a while. Although Jack had made the phone call, they did not rush their dinner. In fact, they even ordered dessert. When they finally left the restaurant and got into the car, the seriousness of the moment started to settle in on both of them. The ride home was a quiet and pensive one. When they arrived at the house, Jack stayed in the car because he was going to find a payphone and call Alice to meet with her.

"Sonny, I'll be home in a while. I just have to call Aunt Alice and meet with her for a short time. I won't be long."

"Okay, Dad. I had a great time tonight, thanks. And dad, I love you."

Sonny got out of the car and headed for the front door. He waved just before he went inside, but Jack had trouble seeing it because of the tears that were welling up in his eyes. He dried his eyes and headed for a payphone where he dialed Alice's number. She immediately answered and thanked Jack for calling. They made arrangements to meet at a local gin mill. Alice wanted to meet in a public place so that Jack would be somewhat restricted in his reaction to what Alice was about to tell him.

Twenty minutes later, Alice and Jack were sitting in a local bar. They ordered drinks, and Alice looked directly at Jack. She started to cry as she knew that she was about to devastate Jack with her news: "Jack I am so sorry!"

Chapter Twenty-Two

They're Killing Me

"Alice, what's wrong? What are you sorry about? Speak to me. Tell me what's on your mind."

In between sobs and catching her breath, Alice relayed to her brother exactly what she had heard. She told him why she wanted to visit Mary, and that she wanted to surprise her sister. She emphasized to Jack that she was the one who was ultimately surprised, no, even shocked. Jack listened carefully, but didn't say anything at all, so Alice just continued speaking and saying whatever came into her mind. She was waiting for the silence to explode into a devastating, ear-splitting yell of disbelief. However, when Jack finally spoke, he asked Alice to repeat, once again, exactly what she had heard. The last thing that Alice wanted to do was to repeat the conversation that she overheard, but Jack's calm silence and focus was more alarming to her than an explosion of anger. To Alice, it seemed like the calm before the storm, but she was not going to test Jack's patience, so she repeated what she had heard.

Still having a hard time believing what he was hearing, Jack needed to clarify what he thought Alice said: "Alice, let me get this straight. You are telling me that when you went to the kitchen to surprise your sister, you saw that she was on the phone and so you waited. Mary didn't realize that you were there, and so, she continued to speak to the person on the other end who you say was Frank. You then say that you heard Mary say to Frank something to the effect that they killed our father. Is that what you're telling me?"

"Yes, Jack that is what I am telling you. I can't believe it either, and I definitely did not want to tell you until I was sure of what I heard, but I went over it again and again in my mind, and I am certain that is what I heard. Jack, please tell me what we are going to do."

"Alice, there is no 'we.' I will take care of things in my own way, and I assure you that our father will rest in peace." At that moment, Jack took out the worn piece of paper that Mary had given him from Antonio and showed it to Alice. It was difficult to make out the message, but she saw the Italian writing and recognized it as her father's. Alice did not understand Italian, so she asked Jack to translate the message for her.

Jack took the message back from Alice and read it; " *Mi stanno uccidendo* 'translates into 'they're killing me.' Dad gave this to Mary to give to me. He knew that I would not rest until I found out what and who he was talking about. Mary never opened it, and if she did, she wouldn't have known what it said. Dad apparently assumed that Frank and Mary were plotting his death, but he couldn't do anything about it. However, Alice, I can. Yeah, it's too late to save our father, but not too late to seek justice and revenge."

Alice became alarmed by Jack's tone and worried about what Jack might be planning. Jack was not yelling in anger, nor threatening violence. No, Alice was sure he was plotting his revenge. He was imagining a plan that would bring his father's murderers to justice, his justice. Jack got up from the table and started pacing in the bar. As he paced, one could tell that he was in deep thought. Alice almost regretted telling Jack what she had heard but didn't want to imagine what Jack would do if he found out that she knew all about this and didn't tell him. So, although frightened and now alarmed, she had no other choice but to alert Jack to what she knew. Her only alternative was to try to reason with Jack and calm the rage that she was sure was building inside of him. She couldn't imagine what he was planning for his sister and brother, but she knew that it would be something that neither one would ever forget nor from which they would ever recover.

Jack stopped his pacing and told Alice that he had to leave and return home to see his son. He had told Sonny that he wouldn't be long, and he didn't want to disappoint him in light of the conversation that had taken place between the two of them. So, he thanked Alice for confiding in him and asked her not to reveal her experience to anyone else. He told her that he would take care of everything, and that he would keep her in the loop. Alice understood and begged Jack not to do anything crazy. She didn't want him to jeopardize his own safety and future. Jack agreed to not react out of pure anger, and that he would consider the fact that the two manipulators were still his brother and sister. Alice was placated by Jack's remarks, and they left the bar going their separate ways.

Before Jack got into his car, he looked to make sure that Alice was out of sight and earshot. He then yelled at the top of his lungs. He had held his frustration and anguish at bay for Alice's benefit, but now he was able to let out his pent-up feelings. He had said things to allay some of the fear that he knew Alice was harboring. He made sure that she thought things would progress slowly and wouldn't be devastatingly damaging to anyone, especially to Mary and Frank. However, he would never let them forget what they had done. They had hastened the demise of a man who supported the family for his entire life. He was a man that only wanted the best for his children. He did everything that he could to make certain that they were all cared for and on their way to better lives. His reward for all his generosity and caring was a plot to speed up his death. No, Jack would not let them get away with the murder of his father.

The plan to expedite Antonio's death reaped the rewards that Frank was expecting. He had numerous meetings with the mob bosses who were grooming him for bigger and better things. The hijacking operation was a total success, and it brought in a lot of money for the family. In the meetings with the bosses, Frank had mentioned how helpful and effective his brother, Michael, had been. He had asked that Michael be considered for a more responsible position, and the family granted Frank that accommodation. In addition to actually driving the stolen trailers to the warehouse, Michael was now the contact man for the distribution of the goods they stole. Michael couldn't be happier, and he took to his new additional position with the determination of a rookie trying out for a major league team.

The responsibilities connected to the mob family took up the majority of Michael's time, and so the attention to the church charges were suffering. He had to cancel a number of meetings with the church elders, and he often couldn't attend the services that were normally routine for him. His wife continued to be as active as possible, but she was no substitute for Michael. Although some would say that his priorities were misplaced, as far as he was concerned, his immediate family was in a better place because of his dealings with the mob. In fact, he was hoping to follow in his brother's footsteps and rise up the organized crime ladder.

Of course, Michael had no idea about what Alice had told Jack, and Michael was so close to Frank now, he probably wouldn't have believed it. Jack tried to keep in touch with Michael as much as he could, and, at times, Jack met with Michael for lunch or a drink. After his meeting with Alice, Jack decided that it was time for another meeting with Michael. He wanted to make sure that Michael was not in so deep that he was blinded to the risks that were apparent in the world of the mafia. Unfortunately, Frank seemed to be Michael's role model, and he encouraged Michael at every turn. It also looked good for Frank that his referral, his brother Michael, was an asset to the mob family. So, it was to Frank's benefit that his brother, Michael, succeeded.

Jack reached out for Michael and arranged for a lunch meeting with him. Jack wanted to see his brother, Michael, for a number of reasons. He wanted to know if Michael was risking too much as he continued working for the mob, but that wasn't the only reason he wanted to meet with his brother. Jack was determined to get back at Frank, and he didn't want Michael to be counted as collateral damage as Jack's plan unfolded. Jack couldn't tell Michael what he was planning, but he could find out how involved Michael was with his brother, and how close they were in the operation. Jack knew that the gifts that the Balaticco family received were the result of the ill-gotten gains of some illegal operation. However, the family never questioned the source since they were the benefactors of whatever their brothers were involved in. The Balaticco family never would have been able to afford many of the items that Frank had brought to them. So, no one asked questions. They just thanked their brother and said nothing.

Jack and Michael met at the local bar that seemed to be the family's meeting place. The bar also served lunch items, so it was a good place to meet. Jack immediately noticed that Michael had matured in a streetwise way. He wasn't that holy roller anymore. He was a guy with responsibilities and charges given to him by organized crime. He even spoke in a different manner. Frank had expedited the situation that their father had hoped would never happen. He had indoctrinated his younger brother into the world of organized crime. But did Frank really care about what his father had wanted? Wasn't he one of the degenerates who killed their father? Jack realized that he was mentally asking rhetorical questions.

"So, Michael, how are things going with your family, and are you still heavily involved with the church?"

"It's good to see you, Jack. Everything is fine with the family. The kids are getting big, and the wife is doing fine. She still gets involved with the church, but I, unfortunately, have other responsibilities that many times interfere with my attendance at church functions. You know, these days, with the price of just ordinary needs, you have to be able to make a good living. And thank God, I am doing okay."

"No, Michael, don' t thank God. I am sure he has nothing to do with organized crime. If thanks are due, and I don't think they should be, it's your brother who should get them. Are you still working with Frank, or have you gone onto bigger and better things?"

"Jack, I think I hear a smattering of sarcasm in your statement. Yeah, I still work with Frank, but I also have some other duties in the operation that I am solely responsible for. It's definitely a step up for me."

"I really don't know if 'congratulations' is the right thing to say or maybe 'what the hell are you doing?' might be better. I know I don't have to tell you this, but when you are involved with the mob, there comes a time when the risk outweighs the reward, and no one even knows when that time comes. Surely, you look at Frank as the model of success, but he is already living on borrowed time. I wouldn't be surprised that in the very near future our family will get a call that he is either in jail or dead. Don't get so involved, Michael, that you can't get out."

"Jack, you sound like the harbinger of doom. Dad was involved, and he never suffered from any calamity. I think if you are careful and don't fight the system, you'll be okay. Don't worry about me, Jack. I have my guardian angel, Frank, watching out for me."

"Sure, dad was involved, but he tried to get out many times. The only way he finally escaped was because he got sick and couldn't perform the way the mob wanted him to. So, he got out, but lived his life looking over his shoulder. Is that what you want?"

"Jack, I don't know what the future holds, but for now, me and my family are happy and living the good life. When the time comes that I want out, I will just go to Frank, and he will smooth the way."

"Michael, you don't know your brother as well as you think you do. If the time comes when you are no longer an asset for him, he wouldn't think twice about eliminating you."

"Jack what are you saying? That he could come right out and kill someone, even a relative."

"No, Michael. You said it!"

Chapter Twenty-Three

A Turn of Events

Although Jack's visit with Michael was not successful in convincing his young brother to separate from the crime family, it was successful in other ways. Jack was smart, and he knew that Michael trusted him. Jack relied on this trust to work out certain information that Michael should never have revealed. However, and because of the implicit trust Michael had in his brother, Jack, he explained the whole hijacking operation so that he could show Jack how really safe he was. Jack was able to ask some pointed questions and was even able to obtain the information that he was looking for. Jack found out when the next scheduled hijacking was going to take place and even how Frank and his group of thugs was given the information. Jack figured that there had to be some internal connection at the Department of Transportation, but he didn't figure it to be two federal agents. At one point, Michael realized that maybe he had offered too much information, so he abruptly changed the subject; however, the damage had already been done. Jack didn't have to press any further, he had what he wanted.

Because he realized that he offered a continuous diatribe about the operation, Michael thought it best that he not even mention to Frank that he had met with Jack. He trusted Jack, but it was foolish to go into such detail just to show Jack that his safety was almost guaranteed. Because of the nature of organized crime, if Frank found out that Michael detailed the operation to Jack, he would definitely come down hard on him. Michael had violated Frank's hard and fast rule to "see everything but say nothing." Michael knew that even though Jack was his brother, the rule still applied with no exceptions. So, since Michael was sure that Jack would do nothing with the information, Michael thought it best just to avoid saying anything to Frank about the meeting. He saw no benefit in creating a rift over something that most likely would amount to nothing.

From the information that Jack had gleaned from Michael, the next scheduled hijacking would not occur for a few weeks. For the most part, this had been the routine. The agents gave Frank and his team plenty of time to prepare. This routine also gave Jack plenty of time to develop a solid plan of action. He would have to make certain that his brother, Michael, was not part of the next scheduled strike.

His vengeance at this point was focused only on Frank and no one else. He would take care of Mary at another time. The difficult part of his plan was getting Michael out from the group that would deliver the hijacking assault. He had to make sure that Michael would not be available to assist with the upcoming scheduled foray. It had to be foolproof so that Frank would have no suspicion that Michael's absence was a planned one.

Jack had a lot of things to think about. In addition to exacting revenge on his brother and sister, he had made the announcement that he was moving out of the house. Marjorie immediately notified Alice and the family, and Jack got the expected deluge of pager notifications, but he was not going to be dissuaded. He made the announcement which vividly brought back the harsh reality of the false premise on which his marriage had been based. He had prepared his son, Sonny, and he was actively looking for a decent apartment which did not cost an arm and a leg. Good apartments were at a premium, so he let everyone know that he was in the market for a decent apartment at a reasonable rent.

After a couple of disappointing weeks, one of Jack's co-workers at "Allure" came to him with news that she knew of an apartment becoming available in the next two weeks. The worker told Jack that the apartment was in the Coney Island area of Brooklyn, and that it was located in the rear yard of a well-known Italian grocery store. By the description, Jack was not enthused about what he was hearing, but he had no other offerings. So, Jack told Lucy, his co-worker, that he would like to see the apartment. Lucy lived with her family in one of the other apartments in the rear yard.

Lucy made the arrangements and after work one evening, Jack met Lucy at the apartment. She introduced Jack to the landlord who was also the owner of the Italian grocery store. After inspecting the apartment, Jack was surprised at how large the rooms were and how well-kept the apartment looked. Since the landlord was close to Lucy's family, and Jack was a referral from Lucy, the landlord gave Jack a discounted price for the rent. Even though Jack was unfamiliar with the Coney Island area, and although the apartment wasn't situated in the best location he had ever seen, he did not hesitate in contracting for the place. The apartment was roomy and well within his price range. He shook hands with the landlord and thanked Lucy for the recommendation. He would move into the apartment within the next few days. That was one thing off his mind.

The date for the trailer assault that Michael had mentioned to Jack was close at hand. Jack had figured out a way to delay Michael from being available the day of the planned hijacking. He had needed the help of the church pastor which was enthusiastically given. Jack and the pastor worked together to make sure that Michael would not be able to meet with the rest of the assault crew. Michael was called to the church basement to help the pastor identify certain items that were found in an abandoned room in the rear of the basement. The room had been sealed off by a huge metal door that the pastor found opened. On the day of the scheduled hijacking, Michael responded to the church, and he had about an hour to spare before he was to meet Frank and the rest of the thugs.

The room was damp and dirty with many different objects that the pastor thought might be germane to the area. He wanted Michael to identify, if possible, those items that might have been associated with the neighborhood. The pastor was not from Bensonhurst, so he needed some local expertise, and Michael was the individual who might be able to help. As Michael looked through the objects in the dimly lit room, the pastor slowly retreated back toward the entrance doorway. The room wasn't a large room, and the pastor wanted to give Michael as much space as he needed.

The pastor was outside of the room when he tripped and fell into the huge metal door that hung at the entrance. His total weight fell against the door and slammed it closed. The pastor had effectively locked Michael in the room. When Michael heard the noise of the door closing, he ran to the door to stop it from locking him inside. He didn't reach the door in time, and the door closed and locked. Since this had been an abandoned room that the church rarely ever used, finding the key for the lock was almost an impossible task. There were many different locations that had to be searched to find the key. The pastor yelled to Michael that he was going to look for the key. Michael only had a short time before he would be late for his meeting with the assault team. He hated not being there, but he knew that Frank could also operate the trailer. However, it was Michael's job to be there, and apparently, he wasn't going to be able to fulfill his commitment to the other team members, and especially to his brother, Frank.

Frank waited to the very last minute before he redesigned the hijacking plan. He was disappointed that Michael didn't show up and more disappointed in the fact that his brother never even called. However, the hijacking operation would go on with or without Michael.

As usual, the eighteen-wheeler arrived at the specified time and location. The crew used the usual maneuvers in stopping the trailer. With guns drawn, two thugs approached the driver while the others went to the rear doors of the truck. As was the routine, the hijackers always checked the inside of the trailer to make certain the cargo was as described by their contacts. Inside of the cab, the potential hijackers were greeted with three individuals armed with semi-automatic weapons. As the other hijackers opened the rear doors, they were also greeted with four additional men also armed with automatic weapons. The hijackers were totally caught off-guard and were quickly subdued. Frank and the other three men were arrested and taken into custody by agents of the Federal Bureau of Investigation.

Frank Balaticco and the other three men were charged with attempted charges of Robbery, Grand Larceny, Grand Larceny Auto, Criminal Possession of Stolen Property, actual Criminal Possession of a Deadly Weapon, and a variety of other lesser charges. Frank's successful hijacking operation came to a sudden and unexpected halt. Now, the hijacking team had to deal with the courts and a potentially very bleak future. Frank, in particular, was facing some very serious decision-making.

For sure, the agents of the Federal Bureau of Investigation would know that the operation couldn't carry on without inside information. They were going to exert whatever pressure they could to find out who the inside contact was. The extent of that pressure would be focused mainly on Frank Balaticco since he was deemed to be the operation leader.

Frank made two phone calls when he was arrested: one to his immediate clandestine contact in the mob family, and the other ironically to his brother, Jack. He would most likely get a lot more help from the mob than from his brother who had nothing but disdain for him. Frank wondered how the feds found out about the operation and the specifics involved in the day's raid. He asked Jack, who was respected and who had a lot of connections, to try and find out who had confided in the F.B.I. Jack said that he would "try his best." However, he finished the rest of that sentence mentally with "to make sure you suffer for what you did to our father!"

With help from the mob, Frank made bail and began his long and arduous fight to try and beat the criminal charges levied against him. Along the way, he was sure that the district attorney's office, in collusion with the F.B.I., would be offering him a deal for his cooperation in outing others who were involved in the criminal undertaking. However, Frank

Balaticco knew better than to make a deal with the feds. Doing that would surely put others inside his organization and those people of interest outside the organization in jeopardy. His fate would be sealed if he betrayed the confidentiality that was a foundational trust block in the building of an organized crime family. He would not test the strength of that commitment!

Chapter Twenty-Four

One Down

When Michael was finally released from his temporary imprisonment, he immediately reached out for his brother, Frank. He was about to offer a very lame excuse for his absence, but he had a tough time contacting his brother. However, after a number of different phone calls, he learned that Frank and his entire team were in the custody of law enforcement. Had it been a coincidence that he was locked in a church room and couldn't make the rendezvous? Was it an act of divine intervention for one who had frequented the church? Or was it a plan to intentionally remove him from an organized law enforcement operation that would result in the arrests of the entire hijacking team? Michael's thoughts leaned toward the latter.

Michael's non-participation in the hijacking attempt brought suspicion on him as to his possible alerting the authorities regarding the planned hijacking. Very few people in organized crime, including Frank, believed in coincidences. Frank was the first to question his brother's absence; however, after an in-depth dive into Michael's whereabouts at the time of the arrests, and a very intensive interview with the pastor of the church, Frank was satisfied that Michael really had nothing to do with what went down. It turned out that Michael had no control over what happened at the church. Although the idea of a coincidence was not high on the list of excuses, in this instance, it seemed to be the correct assumption. After Frank finally accepted the chain of events, he was able to convince the others in the crime family that his brother was, in no way, responsible for what had occurred.

Michael took his escape from arrest as a sign that maybe he should reduce the amount of involvement that he had with the crime family. Although he didn't think it would, the idea of arrest and incarceration scared him. The operation had been going on so smoothly that he couldn't believe how the feds and local law enforcement knew about the scheduled strike. He thought carefully about it, and he came to the same conclusion that Frank and the others had come to - someone on the inside tipped off the cops. He knew that Frank and the others who headed up the family had to suspect everyone as a traitor. They, for sure, would run their own investigation and get to the bottom of this betrayal.

There was another complication that arose from the arrests that took place. The police knew that the hijacking operation could not have been as successful as it had been without help from the inside. They kept constant pressure on Frank and his attorneys to reveal who the inside contact was. However, Frank, on the advice of his lawyer, stayed fast in not revealing anything in relation to inside help. It had been transmitted to the mob and ultimately to Frank that his silence would be rewarded down the road if he "took the rap" for the agents who had been involved. He was promised a good job when he got out of prison and a guarantee that his family would be taken care of. Frank didn't have much of a choice. It was to either accept the clandestine proposal offered to him, or tell all and expect an orchestrated attack on his life. He, of course, chose the former. So, he became immune to the constant attempts by the district attorney and law enforcement to cut a deal and expose the internal connection in the Department of Transportation.

Since Michael was only involved with organized crime in relation to the hijacking operation, he decided to lay low for a while and stay clear of the mob and its undertakings. The thugs who were arrested and who were involved in the trailer hijacking did not name any others who might have been involved in the operation. They had become hard-core mob members, and it was against their nature to "squeal to the cops." So, Michael escaped arrest and prosecution. He decided that since the church had saved him from a fate that would have destroyed him, he would spend more time, like before, participating in church sponsored events. The pastor welcomed him back with opened arms.

Jack followed his brother's trial very closely. It had taken approximately six months before a jury found Frank guilty on all charges. He was sentenced to eight years in Elmira State Prison. Frank would be a recipient of the care New York State afforded to wayward individuals. All during the time that the trial was taking place, Frank was in constant communication with his brother, Jack. Since the mob felt that Frank was responsible for the screw up, the bosses placed it in Frank's hands to find out where the leak was. Frank was depending on Jack to help him find out who had contacted the cops. He had learned that it was an anonymous call to the Federal Bureau of Investigation that started the ball rolling toward the final showdown and the resultant arrests. Frank informed Jack, and emphasized to his brother that the mob was depending on him to right the wrong that had occurred. According to the crime family, Frank needed to find out who the traitor was, and once discovered, to quickly dispatch the individual.

The day quickly arrived when Frank would have to begin his term in prison. Jack was one of the last people to see Frank, and once again, Frank asked Jack if he was any closer to finding out who squealed to the cops. Jack knew that the crime family hadn't made any headway discovering who the traitor was, and he relayed that to Frank. Unfortunately, he also was no closer to the answer. As Frank was escorted to the prison transport vehicle, he yelled out in desperation to Jack: "Jack, do you have any idea whatsoever? Do you have a possible line on who it may be?" Jack looked at Frank and yelled back: "Hey Frank, maybe it's a gift from dad!" Frank wasn't sure he heard and understood what Jack had said, but as he entered the transport vehicle, he thought he saw a nasty smirk on Jack's face.

The anonymous phone call to the law enforcement authorities yielded successful results: one, the death of Antonio Balaticco was, at least, partially avenged with justice being served, and two, Michael Balaticco was disenfranchised from the workings of the organized crime family. This day, Antonio was looking down on the recent events that took place, and he was smiling with satisfaction. Jack could almost feel his father's gratitude, and the affectionate pat on the back.

However, Jack was not through with balancing the scales. There was another person who also contributed to the demise of his father. Mary was just as guilty as her brother, Frank, maybe even more so. She was enjoying life in the house where the Balaticco family had grown up. The house was left to her as a result of her father's death, and she, her husband, and children were experiencing a mortgage-free existence. When Antonio died, for Mary to take legal ownership of the house, she had to sign various legal documents. One of those documents stated that as long as she resided in the home, it would remain hers and hers alone. However, the document also stipulated that in the event that the house was put up for sale, the proceeds of that sale would be divided among all of the remaining siblings. This was not something which Mary or anyone else really took notice of because Mary and her family intended to live out their lives in the Balaticco home.

As a result of his conversations with Alice, Jack was aware that Mary let it be known that she was still disturbed by her father's death. As an act of kindness and concern, Jack decided to visit Mary and offer whatever consolation he could give. He called her and told her that he wanted to visit. Mary always got along with Jack, and she was glad to hear from him. They made arrangements for the visit, and Jack planned to see her within the next few days.

Jack hadn't been to the house in a while, so Mary wanted to clean it up a bit and make a good impression on how well she kept the family treasure. It was an easy task since her husband was a clean freak and hated dirt, dust and especially any type of bug or insect. Mary, therefore, kept a very clean house. She had to if she wanted her husband to reside there. However, with Jack coming, she made an extra special effort to have a good showing.

When Jack arrived at the house, Mary hugged him and gave him a very warm greeting. She was sincerely happy that Jack thought enough of her to arrange for a visit and try to reduce some of the grief that she had felt about her father's death. Mary prepared coffee, and Jack opened the tray of cookies that he brought with him. The afternoon went well, and before they knew it, the kids were coming home from school, and Mary had to start preparing for dinner. Although she invited Jack to stay for dinner, he politely refused and said that he would welcome the invitation at another time.

Before he left, Jack went into the bathroom. In the bathroom, he took out a sealed plastic bag from his pants pocket. The creatures inside the bag were restless and jumping around. Jack looked at the bag and smiled as he opened it and dumped the contents on the bathroom floor. As Jack opened the bathroom door, a number of little critters scattered to the different corners of the room and out of the bathroom. A lucky group of cockroaches had found a new home.

As Jack said "good-bye," Mary's kids were coming through the front door. They exchanged their quick "hellos," and Jack was on his way. He had "consoled" Mary as much as he could; but in the near future, it was Jack's strong belief that Mary was going to need a lot more consolation than anyone could possibly offer.

Chapter Twenty-Five

Escape to the Military

A few days had passed, and Jack was in the thick of moving into his new apartment. He had more things than he anticipated moving, but he had help from his brother, Michael, and some of his co-workers. As he continued to take items into the apartment, Jack ran into one of Lucy's brothers who lived in an adjacent apartment. Tommy was the oldest of Lucy's brothers, and he welcomed Jack to the neighborhood. In fact, Tommy pitched in and helped Jack move into the apartment. An instant friendship developed, and for Jack, it made the transition a much easier one.

One of the first things that Jack did after settling in was to invite his son to see the apartment. Jack wanted to bring his son into the whole transition, and he wanted Sonny to feel comfortable visiting his dad. It was kind of odd for Sonny to be in a place that served to separate his father from the family home where they all had lived together as one. However, Sonny knew that this was a long time in coming, and he accepted it for what it was. He knew that his father wanted to maintain the close relationship that they had, and he was going to make that as easy as he could for him. So, he put it into his mind that he was going to get used to visiting the apartment and sometimes even staying there.

When Sonny arrived home from his visit with his father, he was confronted with a deluge of questions from his mother who never really believed that Jack would actually leave. The questions ranged from how the apartment looked to what kind of neighbors Jack had. Sonny felt so bombarded that at one point he told his mother that if she had any more questions, that she should ask his father directly. It was bad enough that Sonny had mixed emotions about his father moving out, he definitely didn't need to be part of his mother's inquisition. He left his surprised mother standing in the kitchen, and he went into his room and cried. His emotions finally got the best of him, and everything he had been holding inside came flooding to the surface. He loved both his parents, and now he had to face the reality of living a separate life with each one.

When Sonny visited the rest of his large family with his mother, he felt how close his mother was to all of them. Instead of his father having his own family as a strong support group, it seemed to Sonny that the family favored his mother even though she was the one who was ultimately responsible for the situation in which he found himself. His aunts always greeted his mother as a long-lost relative who they hadn't seen for years. It was so animated that it appeared to be superficial, an exaggeration of the situation which was geared to exonerate his mother from any responsibility for what had occurred. Although he still loved his mother, this experience in theatre drama only served to push Sonny closer to his father. He felt that all of the antics that took place were being presented with him in mind. It didn't help their cause, and it only it served to bring the reason for the separation to the forefront. Sonny reacted accordingly, and he reluctantly played their silly game.

As time went on, Jack got even closer to his neighbors, and they began to include him in their family happenings. From the very get-go, Jack introduced himself as Dominic Balaticco. He wanted to leave that other life and divorce himself from the name that Marjorie had suggested. So, all of his new acquaintances knew him as Dominic. He became quite close to his neighbors and was even closer to Tommy. Tommy was a member of the local Coney Island Social Club. The club sponsored dances and a number of different social events. Dominic was always invited to attend. The friendliness and concern of his newfound friends were a major asset in Dominic's acclimation to his new place in life.

As Dominic attended more and more social club events, he began to take special interest in one of Tommy's sisters, Gina. It was apparent that the interest was reciprocal, and Tommy also noticed the interaction. Although Dominic was thirteen years older than Gina, she had been married once before and was a mother to her young daughter, Linda. Because of the fact that Gina had been married, Tommy said nothing about the age difference. Had Gina not been married, there would have been major problems for Dominic. Her previous matrimonial situation apparently short-circuited the age difference problem for Gina's older brother. Gina and Dominic began to date exclusively, and Dominic got along very well with Gina's daughter.

As he promised, Dominic stayed close to his son. He spent as much time as possible with him, but Sonny was still having a difficult time dealing with the whole situation. There were a number of things that were affecting his life, and he didn't know how to effectively deal with them. He had been close to his Uncle Frank, but that was now a moot point, and he missed seeing his father every day. He also began to resent his mother for putting the family in disarray, and he couldn't accept the fact that his mother intentionally hurt his father. Sonny also could no longer accept the false front that the Balaticco family always presented to make his mother appear in a favorable light. Sonny knew that he was not college material, so when the time came, he announced to everyone that he was going to enlist in the United States Navy. This decision afforded him two very significant advantages: he would be able to leave behind all the turmoil that he was feeling, and his life would have some direction, at least for four years.

His announcement was greeted with mixed feelings; however, he was not going to be dissuaded from his decision. He had two of his cousins who had already enlisted in the navy, and so that influenced his choice of service. Before he informed the entire family, he had contacted his father to tell him first. Dominic appreciated the fact that his son made a special effort to put him first, but Dominic couldn't escape the idea that his son was joining the navy as a result of what had occurred in the family. He felt guilty that his son had to resort to enlistment to get away from the family discord. However, even though Dominic assured his son that things would get better, Sonny was not going to be swayed from his present course. Dominic understood and gave his son his blessing for a safe and beneficial journey into the United States military. He was going to miss his son, but he only wanted the best for him, and according to Sonny this was definitely the best option for him.

The day that Sonny left for the navy was one of the few times that Dominic and Marjorie were together in the same place. And although it felt odd, it gave a strong send off to their son. There had been a lot of water that flowed under the bridge since Dominic had left, but the angst and anger between the two parents seemed to have calmed somewhat. They were actually civil with one another as they realized that the one person who continued to thread a simple bond between them was now leaving for places unknown. In that moment, they shared the concern, worry, and yearning that all parents felt when a situation pulled at the heartstrings of one's being. By their presence, they almost consoled one another, and as their son looked back, he saw a joint regard that had been absent for some years. Although he had some doubts, now that his departure was imminent, Sonny left with a warm feeling in his heart and a growing confidence that he had done the right thing.

Marjorie and Dominic smiled at one another, both holding back the tears. They went their separate ways, but didn't turn away in anger or disgust, but in mutual concern for how the other was feeling. They knew that they had bid "good-bye" to their young boy, and realized that when he returned, they would be greeted by a young man.

Although Dominic no longer lived in the neighborhood, he felt most comfortable in the local bar that had always served as the unofficial meeting place for his family. He greeted the bartender who was sincerely glad to see him. They exchanged some brief comments, and then Dominic ordered a drink. He stayed in the bar for about an hour or so, and just before he was ready to leave, he heard his name: "Jack? Is that you? What are you doing here?" Jack was face to face with Mary's husband, John, of whom he was not particularly fond. He was shocked that such a germaphobe would patronize such a dismal and dirty place like a bar.

"Hi John, I'm shocked to see you here? I didn't realize that you frequented bars knowing your feelings toward cleanliness. What brings you to the bar?"

"First of all, congratulations on your son joining the navy. I am sure he will excel in the military. It is not often that I come to the bar, but when I feel totally frustrated and disturbed, I find some comfort in a nice drink, and the solitude that the bar offers me."

"What's up, John? You look like a fidgety wreck? Is my sister causing you grief?"

"No, Jack," Dominic interrupted his brother-in-law and told him that he no longer responded to the name "Jack."

"Okay, Dominic, I got you. Your sister is not causing me grief, but the house is definitely pushing me over the edge."

"I don't understand, John. You are living in a mortgage-free world with a house that is in relatively good shape. What could possibly be wrong?"

"Dominic, have you any idea how invasive and prolific a New York cockroach is?"

Chapter Twenty-Six

Like a Lightning Bolt

Sal and Joe had escaped suspicion in the hijacking operation of the crime family. Frank Balaticco took the entire rap for what went down. The other three participants received much lighter sentences since Frank was deemed to be the leader of the group. Frank would have to serve the majority of his sentence but would be rewarded by his associates when he was finally free. As promised, his family would be taken care of while he was away, and he would get a well-paying, good job upon his release from prison.

Michael was truly affected by what was happening to his brother. He felt extremely sad that Frank was going to be imprisoned for approximately eight years, but Michael couldn't escape the relief that he felt knowing that he would still remain a free man. He went over that day's events many times, and really couldn't decide if it was just coincidence that kept him from participating in the events that led to his brother's arrest, or if it was a well-planned strategy to make certain that he would not be present when the arrests went down. However, if it was a plan, then someone knew in advance that the police had been notified, and that someone probably was responsible for making the anonymous phone call to the authorities.

Michael was pretty sure that the pastor was not the one who anonymously notified the police because the pastor would not have known that the hijacking was going to take place on that day. Michael racked his brain as to whom outside of the group knew that there was a hijacking planned. For obvious reasons, Michael was sure that no one involved in the operation would put themselves in jeopardy, so, in his opinion, it had to be someone who knew the schedule and would not be negatively affected. It would also be someone who wanted the operation to end in arrests and jail time, but someone who didn't want Michael counted as having anything to do with the hijacking operation.

Like a bolt of lightning hitting him directly in the chest, Michael's thoughts went to the only person to whom he had mentioned the upcoming operational specifics. He had lunch with his brother, Jack, and as he recalled the conversation, he had mentioned the operation and the specifics of the next assault. Michael shook his head, not wanting to admit that Jack could very well be the individual who was responsible for the entire disaster that befell Frank and his team. Michael was aware that Jack was not in favor of his youngest brother's involvement in organized crime operations, but it had to be more than that before Jack would take such an extreme action that would undoubtedly result in the incarceration of another brother. Michael had to find out for sure before the burning in his stomach led to an even greater malady. He reached out for his brother, Jack.

Jack had listened carefully as Mary's husband, John, went on about what was plaguing the former home of the Balaticco family. He mentioned that these huge bugs came out of nowhere and were infiltrating all parts of the house. He told Dominic that he couldn't stay in the house because of his extremely negative affinity to dirt, dust, insects, and the like. He said that he temporarily rented an apartment until the house could be free of the invasion. The house had been fumigated once already, but, as John related, cockroaches were apparently very enduring bugs, and the fumigation was unsuccessful. He mentioned that they were going to have the house fumigated one more time in the hope that a double dose would eliminate the problem. However, until there was a sign of success, John was going to remain in the apartment that he rented. He also mentioned that if the second fumigation failed, the only alternative left was to sell the house.

Dominic played his role very well. He showed sincere concern and distress over what John and Mary were experiencing. He offered to help in any way that he could, but they both realized that there was nothing that anyone could do but to wait for the results of the second fumigation. As Dominic inquired as to the rest of John's family, Dominic's always busy pager started to beep. When he looked at the screen, it showed that his brother, Michael, was reaching out to him. Because Michael was so obviously affected by what happened to his brother, Frank, and the fact that he was miraculously saved from the situation, Dominic wondered if Michael had come to some conclusion about how it all went down. However, because Dominic was involved with John at the moment, he chose to contact Michael later on. He could only deal with one problem at a time.

Alice was an intelligent young woman, and she had a knack for analyzing and evaluating situations. When everything originally went south regarding Frank and the hijacking operation, her thoughts immediately went to her brother, Jack. She remembered the look on Jack's face as she revealed to him that she had heard her sister admit to being involved in their father's death. It was not a look of total hate or rage, but rather one that expressed cunning and justice for Antonio's premature demise.

So, now when Mary had contacted her and expressed the marital problems she was having because of an infestation that came out of nowhere, Alice's antennae went up and, once again, her brother, Jack, came to mind. Could it be that Jack had something to do with this unexplainable occurrence? Mary was at her wits end, and she only had a second fumigation application as a last resort for solving the problem. Alice tried to console Mary by telling her that she was sure that a second fumigation would solve the problem, but in her heart, she wasn't sure that it would. Cockroaches were a hardy group, and they had been around since the stone age.

When she finished speaking with her sister, Alice wanted to satisfy her curiosity, so she dialed Jack's work number. She tried a number of times but was unable to get through. As she tried another way, Jack's pager rang in the bar as he was talking with John. When Jack looked at his screen this time, he saw Alice's number come up. He wondered if she had been speaking with Mary. He knew that Alice might connect him to the bad luck that befell his brother, Frank, and now she might have some thoughts about how a cockroach invasion had targeted Mary's home. Once again, Jack did not want to interrupt his conversation with John, so he didn't answer the page. Because of the two pages that came one right after the other, John commented that Dominic seemed to be a very busy guy. In fact, Dominic was. He had a lot of things going on at work, and he had a number of situations going on in his family.

Dominic ended the conversation with John on the note that he would be contacting Mary and offering any help that she might need. John was thankful for Dominic's concern as he ordered another drink. Dominic left, not with a smile on his face, but what could possibly be described as a sneer. He would definitely call his sister, Mary, because he would revel in the fact that she was beside herself with worry. She deserved what she got and more. He was almost positive that a second shot at fumigation would not lead to a resolution of the problem, and if Mary wanted to save her marriage, she would have to put the house up for sale and move. He was also sure that Mary didn't consider the option of moving a bad one. The house was paid up, and its sale would command a decent amount of money. With the proceeds from the sale, she, John and her family would start a new life in an even better house. However, as Dominic assumed, Mary never read the documents that she signed when she took over the house. She was totally unaware of the conditions that applied once the house was sold. By contrast, Dominic was keenly aware of them.

Dominic had to answer the pages by both Michael and Alice. He had trouble deciding which would respond to first. With Michael, Dominic would never admit to being a part of a conspiracy to destroy his brother, Frank. However, Michael might potentially be able to infer from Dominic's comments that there was a strong possibility that his older brother had a significant role in the ultimate incarceration of his brother, Frank. Dominic realized that this absorbed inference would surely cause a schism in his relationship with the youngest brother in the family. However, the positive results of Michael being a free man were well worth the hardship of a strained relationship which, in time, would mend.

When it came to speaking with Alice, it was going to be difficult for Dominic not to imply or have her infer any possible incriminating connection to the two events. She was smart enough to see through any charade, so Dominic decided to be straight up with his sister, Alice. She might not agree with the tactics that Dominic used in both occurrences, but she was definitely in agreement with the fact that both her sister, Mary, and her brother, Frank, should be held accountable for what they did. And when she told Dominic what she had heard, she knew that he would be the instrument, the person, who would avenge their father's death. So, Dominic, already knowing Alice's stance on his actions, chose to call her first.

Chapter Twenty-Seven

Facing the Music

Dominic, having been out of the house now for the past six months, took positive action and filed for divorce. It was foolish for anyone to believe that the separation would bring them closer together. In Dominic's mind, nothing would do that. He had made up his mind, and as far as he was concerned, it was final. Additionally, there was no rush on Marjorie's side to want to work things out. She had no feelings for Dominic, and it seemed that she was also enjoying her freedom. So, Dominic, before long, had successfully divorced himself from any further connection to his one-time wife, Marjorie.

The divorce was completed while Sonny was away, and when he was notified that a divorce was finalized, he was not shocked or surprised. He had known for a while that entertaining the thought that there was a possibility of a reunion was just wishful thinking. He witnessed, firsthand, how strained his parents' relationship had been, so Sonny took the news in stride and told his parents that he understood why a divorce followed the natural progression of their separation. Although he let them know that he understood and accepted what had transpired, he also let them know that he was somewhat disappointed about how things worked out. Any child hates to see their parents separating and going their own way, and Sonny was no different. He didn't let any of his fellow sailors see, but when he got the notification, tears welled up in his eyes. He knew that sooner or later it was coming, but when it finally did, reality punched him right in the gut. The union that his parents had once formed was now permanently dissolved. Sonny felt better that he was away when getting the news, rather than having to face his parents when reality hit.

There was another reason why Dominic pushed for divorce. He and Gina were getting serious, and Dominic wanted to face the future with a clean slate. If his relationship with Gina was to go forward and develop into something that became a lifelong commitment, he didn't want something like a lingering past association mudding up the waters. He was now free, and he no longer had debilitating baggage to carry forward. Additionally, he would allay some of the concerns that Gina's older brother, Tommy, had. Dominic had spoken to Tommy a couple of times about his intentions, and Tommy had indicated that things would go a lot smoother if Dominic cut all ties with his former wife. The fact that Dominic was going to be a divorcee, however, was not a problem since Gina had also divorced from her husband, Linda's father.

Dominic had been getting along very well with Linda. She took to him, and he had no problem taking on the role of a substitute dad. Apparently, Linda's father wanted nothing to do with his child, so he never came around. This made Dominic's connection with the little girl even easier and more significant. Also, Gina was elated that her little girl looked to Dominic as someone to whom she could relate as a parent, and as far as Dominic was concerned, he welcomed the warmth and satisfaction he got from their interactions.

Dominic finally took the bull by the horns and returned Alice's page. He dialed her number and prepared himself for the accusations that he was sure would be forthcoming. He wasn't going to attempt to deny his involvement in his brother's and sister's turmoil, but he also wasn't going to elaborate or dwell on the satisfaction that he felt as a result of his actions.

"Hello, Jack." As he did with his brother-in-law, he interrupted Alice to let her know that he no longer answered to the name "Jack," and that he went back to his baptismal name of Dominic. Alice being Alice answered: "I don't care what you call yourself these days, I'm just interested in speaking to you about what has occurred in the lives of both Frank and Mary. Jack, (she apparently didn't care about what her brother had said regarding the name change) no matter what you are about to tell me, I know that you had something to do with the hardships and problems that both Frank and Mary are facing. Frank is in jail, and Mary most likely will have to move out of the house, and maybe lose her husband in the interim. Jack, do you care to explain?"

"Alice, when you told me what you had heard, I immediately decided that our sister and brother would pay for what they did. You shouldn't be surprised about anything that happens to either one of them. You knew that I was going to balance the scales. I seem to remember that you were worried about how drastic a response I would have regarding the news that you relayed to me. In my opinion, what I have done is far from drastic. It is just a little communication from dad telling them that he knew what they had done, and that their selfishness and greed only served to introduce them to the potential hardships that life sometimes has to offer."

"Jack, stop the bullshit. You sent our brother to jail."

"Alice, hold on a minute. You don't get it, do you? He, with help from Mary, murdered our father. He should be serving a life sentence. They are both criminals. Don't you lecture me about how I avenged our father's death. As far as I am concerned, they both got off easy. We cannot undo what they have done, and we will never see our father again. They have inflicted irreparable harm on our entire family, and a loss from which we will never recover!"

Alice was taken aback by the severity and directness of Jack's tone. She almost felt like she was being chastised for what she said. So, she decided to tone down her response and bring calm into the conversation: "Jack, I realize what they have done is unforgiveable, but they will suffer from what you did to them for the rest of their lives. Maybe, they deserve it, but I can't divorce myself from the fact that they are still our siblings. It bothers me that they will never recover from your actions. I know that I can do nothing to mitigate their hardship, but I am telling you now that I will help them as much as I can."

"Alice, you have to do what you have to do; however, when you are helping them cope with their problems, remember that they fed our father the poison that took his life. They are killers, murderers who put themselves before all else even if it meant eliminating a life and hurting everyone else in the process. But Alice, you do whatever you have to do!"

Before Alice could say anything else, Dominic hung up. The call had gone worse than he anticipated, and he was bothered by the outcome. That was supposed to be the easier of the calls that he had to make. He hesitated before he returned Michael's page. He was somewhat reeling from the conversation he had with Alice.

He took a few deep breaths and dialed Michael's number. To his relief, the call went straight to the answering machine, so he didn't have to enter into any type of banter with his younger brother, at least not for now. He went over the conversation that he had with Alice, and he couldn't believe how she was putting Antonio's death to the back burner in favor of helping her brother and sister cope with their problems. Dominic felt that she was missing the entire point of avenging their father's death. Didn't she realize that they took something from the family that could never be replaced? Didn't she realize that if they went the way of the law, that Frank and Mary would be experiencing a much greater punishment? Didn't she realize they both put themselves first, in front of everyone else in the family and didn't look back? As Dominic was pondering all of these questions, his pager, once again, beeped. Michael was returning his call. He dialed Michael's number again.

"Hello, Michael. How are you doing? Is everything okay?"

"You know, Jack, I really don't know if everything is okay." As he had done twice before, Dominic interrupted the conversation and inserted the fact that he no longer answered to the name "Jack," and that he only used his baptismal name of Dominic.

It was apparent that no matter how many times he was going to tell his family not to call him "Jack," they would continue with the name. There were three obvious reasons why this occurred: one, they had been used to calling him "Jack," two, it was their way of respecting Marjorie, and three, they knew that Gina hated the name and reference.

"Jack, I mean Dominic, when did this happen? For all these years you called yourself 'Jack,' and now, all of a sudden, you are 'Dominic'."

"It's a long story, Michael, but please call me 'Dominic'."

"You got it. I imagine you are calling to return my page. I have something on my mind, and I can't seem to clear it up. It has been bothering me for some time now. You know that I was coincidentally delayed the day that Frank and the crew ran into the police. And from what I have gleaned, the police received an anonymous call about the operation. I have been racking my brain, as I am sure you have, trying to determine who would have made the call. I gave it a lot of thought, and it had to be someone who was privy to the operation and the schedule of the hijacking. Of course, it wouldn't be someone who was actually involved in the assault because that would also put them in jeopardy, so it had to be someone who would remain free from any repercussion. Dominic, I started thinking about who could possibly know where and when the hijacking would take place. Dominic, you knew."

"So, what does that mean, Michael? Because I knew some of the details, I was the one who called the police. Is that what you are saying, Michael? You're implying that I would put Frank and you in danger."

"No, Jack. You probably arranged for the pastor to help out and lock me in that Godforsaken basement room. You made sure that your youngest brother was out of harm's way and would not suffer the consequences of potential arrest and jail time. Believe me, I am thankful that I do not have to vegetate in the confines of a prison cell, but I can't accept an action that would put one of our family members behind bars. Now, I know that Frank has no idea that you might be the culprit who set him up, but I am at a loss to think of anyone else. So, Dominic, tell me that I am way off base and suffering from some hallucinogenic mental distortion."

There was an uncomfortable silence for a while, and then Dominic spoke directly to Michael and said: "If it took an extreme measure to save a life, would you do it? Let me answer for you. You would. If it meant that you could balance the scales for a life that was taken unjustly, would you go to the extreme to do it? You would. Would you make a sacrifice to ensure that a heinous act which took a life, was, at least partially, avenged? You would. Michael, so would I!"

Michael seemed a little confused, but he wasn't sure if he wanted Dominic to explain further. There was a strong implication that his brother, Frank, might have been involved in some dire activity that had to deal with taking the life of another human being. If that was the case, Michael didn't want to know the details. Although he took Dominic's comments to heart, he answered accusatorily to Dominic and said: "I am sure that Frank would not agree with the fact that you appointed yourself as judge, jury and executioner, and I hope, for your sake, that he never finds out that you dictated his fate. I can only look at you now with prejudiced eyes."

"Michael, I mentioned the concept of a life taken. Someday, when the time is right, and you are able to accept what I have had to internalize for a long while, I will let you know some significant details that will, unfortunately, force you to reconsider what you are feeling now."

"Dominic, nothing will change the way I look at you now. When will it be my turn that you decide to judge my actions and turn against me? Dad would be turning over in his grave right now."

"Michael, he already has!"

Chapter Twenty-Eight

Antonio Finally Smiles

As he promised John, Mary's husband, Dominic reached out to Mary. To say the least, she was in a very bad way. She told Dominic that she had tried everything to solve her problem with the house but was unable to reach a positive result. Her last shot was coming up with a second fumigation. She mentioned to Dominic that if the fumigation failed again, that she would have to consider selling the house. She did not want to sell since the house had been in the family forever, but she was left with no other choice.

"I wouldn't worry about it, Mary. I'm sure that the second application by the exterminator will be successful. Those chemicals are very strong and applying them twice can't help but be successful."

"I hope you're right, Jack, because besides the problems with the house, my marriage is also suffering. John is very strange about things like this, and he sometimes acts spontaneously. This whole situation could well result in a possible separation. That would be horrible. I don't know what I would do without John being there."

"I wouldn't worry about it now, Mary. Let's wait to see what happens with the fumigation. Oh, by the way, I don't use the name, 'Jack' anymore. Please call me Dominic."

"What happened? Why not 'Jack'?"

"It's a long story, Mary. Just call me by my baptismal name. When is the exterminator scheduled to apply the second dose of chemicals?"

"The exterminator will be here tomorrow early in the morning. We will be staying at Frank's place with Colleen for the day until the fumes dissipate. I am praying that those nasty creatures all die. I want to get back to normal living back home with my children and my husband."

"Okay, Mary. I will give you a call tomorrow to see how things went. I am sure that after tomorrow, things will return to normal. Mary, not that it will happen, but what's your next move if things don't change?"

"Ja.., Dominic, if the fumigation doesn't get rid of the bugs, I will have to get rid of the house. It's not what I want to do, but I'll have no choice. Selling the house will kill me. It's been in our family forever. That having been said, I am sure it will bring a very decent price. We will have to start over, and with the money we get from the sale, I am sure that we will be able to find something that is even more than suitable for us. I am hoping, however, to stay right where we are."

As Dominic listened to Mary's plans if and when the fumigation failed, the same sneer that appeared on his face after speaking with Mary's husband, John, arose again. Whether the exterminator was successful or not, the fumigation was going to fail. Dominic would make sure of it, even if it meant that he would visit with another plastic bag filled with those "indestructible" cockroaches. One way or the other, Mary was going to put her house up for sale, not being aware of the fact that profit from the sale would have to be divided among all of the siblings. Dominic just couldn't wait to exact "revenge, sweet revenge."

"Okay, Mary, I will be in touch with you tomorrow. If you find out anything before I call, please let me know. Talk to you soon." Dominic hung up with his sister and imagined Mary screaming when she saw the first cockroach again. The sneer appeared again.

The Balaticco family found out that their brother, Dominic, was serious about someone he had met in his new neighborhood. The family, especially Alice, did not take this well. No matter what, they favored Marjorie. Again, the family was treating the entire situation as if Marjorie were the offended party and Dominic the offender. They totally turned against their brother, and therefore, they would be against anyone with whom Dominic became involved.

Dominic was not immune to the situation, and although he tried to mitigate their prejudiced view, his efforts always fell on deaf efforts. Because of this, Dominic waited as long as he could before he brought Gina to a family gathering and introduced her to his family. He actually dreaded the introduction, but Gina had been asking for a while to meet his family. He was more than aware of how the females in the family, led by the outspoken, self-centered, rebel, Alice, would react in defense of their favorite, Marjorie. He didn't know how he was going to explain in advance to Gina that her meeting with his family meant, through no fault of her own, that she was entering into hostile territory. By way of telling Gina that Marjorie was well-liked by his family, he tried to imply that winning them over would be no easy task. In fact, Dominic wasn't sure if they would ever change their stance and welcome someone new with open arms. Gina understood where Dominic was coming from and let him know that she was no shrinking violet. She would take things as they came. Dominic applauded his girlfriend's attitude but felt that she was underestimating Alice and the girls.

Dominic, at the constant nudging of Gina, called Alice and made arrangements for the family to meet his new girlfriend. Alice was more than obliging and said that she would invite whoever was available to come to her house on the scheduled date and time. To Dominic, it seemed that Alice was more than receptive to the idea, and that she couldn't wait. All Dominic saw were danger signs and alarms going off. Alice was too receptive, and since the date was a week away, it gave her plenty of time to plan.

After his call to Alice, Dominic couldn't emphasize enough to Gina that they were walking into the lion's den. Gina tried to allay some of Dominic's fears by telling him that some sort of resistance was to be expected, and that she understood their concern, especially having to deal with the fact that she was fourteen years younger than he. The age difference alone was a point of controversy. Dominic just shook his head and thought that Gina didn't know what his family was capable of. Two of them had hastened their father's death, and they now favored an individual who had deceived their brother with total disregard for his feelings. He wished that he could blink his eyes and make it all go away, but Gina was gung-ho.

On the scheduled day, the exterminator came as promised. Mary and the kids left for the day and let the exterminator do his work and fumigate the entire house. He almost guaranteed that the problem would be solved with the second application of the chemicals. Mary left feeling good about the situation, and decided to contact her husband to let him know that the exterminator was at the house and potentially solving the problem.

John was receptive to the news but warned that if the problem wasn't solved, they would have to resort to the only option left to them, selling the house. Mary understood and placated John by telling him that she would have no problem selling the house if fumigation failed. Although John was paranoid about the bugs, she too wasn't exactly happy about sharing their residence with the ugly creatures that had invaded their home. She would sell the house without ever looking back. She dwelled on the fact that the whole thing might be a blessing in disguise. They would have money to invest in a bigger and better house located in a more affluent neighborhood. So, either way, her immediate family were winners, and she would have her husband back.

Dominic waited until evening on the next day after the fumigation before he contacted Mary. He called in the early evening and heard the joy and relief in Mary's voice. She said that she couldn't wait to tell him that her problems were over. When she went back to the house, both her and the exterminator did a thorough inspection of the house and found no trace of any bug infestation. The second fumigation apparently succeeded in eliminating the onslaught of cockroaches. Dominic outwardly joined in the satisfaction of defeating the bugs. He told Mary that he was going to bring a bottle of champagne over to the house and celebrate with her and her husband. Mary welcomed the idea of celebrating with her brother and told him to come over on the following night. John was also enthused to celebrate the relief in having a clean house and getting back to living a normal family life.

The next evening saw Dominic, champagne in hand, visiting Mary and John. They were more than happy to see Dominic, and the celebration began immediately. It seemed to Dominic that the celebration had begun well before his arrival. Mary had prepared some hors d'oeuvres, and the threesome ate and drank until midnight. Everyone relayed how relieved they were and what might have been the unfortunate alternative if the problem had not been solved. Mary exclaimed a number of times how saddened she would have been if they had been forced to adopt the only option that was left open to them. They all agreed that the house remaining in the family was a welcome result.

As it got increasingly later in the evening, Dominic mentioned that he had his fill of champagne and wine and that he, unfortunately, had to call his participation in the evening's celebration to an end. John and Mary understood, and they agreed to terminate the festivities. So, as usual, Dominic paid a visit to the bathroom before he left. As he did the first time, he introduced unwelcomed visitors into the house. Dominic reached into his pants pocket and came out with a plastic bag of crawling cockroaches. He sprinkled them on the bathroom floor and placed some under the bathroom door which led out into the kitchen where John and Mary were sitting. Dominic gave it sometime before he left the bathroom. He allotted enough time for the cockroaches to invade the kitchen. Although only two of them reached the kitchen, Dominic heard the screams and ran out of the bathroom.

"What's wrong? I heard the screams, what's happening?"

Without uttering a word, both John and Mary pointed at the cockroach meandering across the kitchen floor. Demonstrating shock and surprise, Dominic put his hand over his mouth and uttered: "Oh, no!"

Mary started crying and John was close to climbing on the kitchen table. The celebration ended in disaster. Mary turned to Dominic and shouted: "What do we do now? I can't believe that they are still here. Dominic, I don't understand. Where could they have come from?"

Dominic hesitated for a short time and then answered in the same way as he did with his brother, Frank: "Maybe, it was a gift from dad." Dominic's half-smile resembled that familiar sneer, but he shrugged his shoulders in what appeared to be total despair. He mumbled to Mary that he would be in touch. The sneer appearing again, Dominic turned and left.

Chapter Twenty-Nine

She Held Her Own

The time arrived, and Dominic prepared himself for the worst. He and Gina were going over to Alice's house where the rest of the family had gathered for the special introductory event. Dominic tried to prepare Gina as best he could, but she just waved him off like it was no big deal. Again, Dominic worried that she was underestimating the Balaticco family. He figured that the welcoming contingent would consist mostly of his sisters since the guys really didn't have that much input into something of this nature. If the relationship continued, however, then down the road, the guys would meet their brother's other half.

On the way to Alice's house, there was nervous small talk in the car. It was mostly Dominic who did the talking. He was a lot more anxious than Gina, and he figured that she was calmer because she really didn't know the women of the Balaticco family. Maybe, it was better that way. Why be affected by nerves when you didn't have to be? Sure, there was some apprehension in meeting a totally new group of people, but there were no added nervous complications. As far as Gina was concerned, after the initial awkwardness of meeting new people had passed, the meeting would go on as if they had known each other forever. Gina conveyed this thinking to Dominic who just shook his head in disbelief as to how naive Gina was regarding the jackals who awaited their arrival.

Alice couldn't have timed it better. As Dominic parked the car and escorted Gina up the front stairs to the entrance door, the door opened, and there was Marjorie face-to-face with both of them. There was awkward silence until Dominic broke the spell by recognizing Marjorie: "Hello, Marjorie. How are you doing?" Before his ex-wife could answer, he introduced Gina to Marjorie. They both nodded and said "hello." Dominic and Gina had not even entered the house, and the "fun" had begun. Dominic forced a hurried "good-bye" to Marjorie, and ushered Gina into the house. As he passed Alice, he gave her a look that promised repercussions.

When Marjorie first saw Dominic, she called him "Jack." That name was foreign to Gina who only knew her boyfriend as "Dominic." As the other family members greeted the couple, they also referred to him as "Jack." This was in total conflict to what Dominic had mentioned to the family. He told them all that he did not want to be called "Jack" any longer, and that he would respond to "Dominic." The difference in name was confusing to Gina, but she didn't question it right away. She decided to put off the inquiry until things got a little lighter in the room. The introductions went off without a hitch, and to Dominic's surprise, Michael was also in the room.

For the better part of the evening, Dominic was surprised at how well things were going. That was the case until a discussion about Dominic's son came up. Alice made sure that Gina knew that Dominic had left his wife and son when Sonny was only sixteen years old. And, of course, Alice heavily implied that the teen years were the period when a young boy most needs his father. Gina agreed with Alice but added that she was aware that the father-son bond was as strong as ever.

Dominic was pleased with Gina's response, but he knew that Alice would not be so easily thwarted. Alice asked if Gina knew that Sonny had enlisted in the United States Navy. Of course, Gina and Dominic had discussed his son, and Gina was aware that Sonny had enlisted. When Alice heard the affirmative response from Gina, she went into attack mode: "Gina, do you know why Sonny decided to enlist and not go to college or look for a local job? Do you know why he decided to separate from his family for the next four years? Do you know why he felt better being away from his mother and father than being with them?" Not only were

Alice's questions focused and pointedly self-serving, but her tone implied that there were some serious background facts to which Gina, most probably, had not been privy.

When Alice finished her barrage of questions, there was silence in the room. Everyone had known that at one point in the social gathering, Alice would let her feelings be known. They were just unaware of how she would frame them. Apparently, they were couched in a deluge of accusatory questions aimed at Dominic's lack of parenting and concern for his family, especially for his son, Sonny. The family knew that Alice was not yet done, and that she would definitely have some follow-up. However, they were also expecting an outburst from Dominic to put Alice in her place. He was about to speak when he felt a strong squeeze on his hand. Gina was signaling to him that she would take care of the present matter. He reluctantly sat back and waited for Gina's retort.

Gina took a few seconds to digest all of what Alice had said, and what she had implied. Then Gina spoke in a calm but authoritative voice, a voice to which Dominic was totally unfamiliar: "Alice, I appreciate the questions that you brought to light in an effort, I'm sure, to allow me to know what possible pitfalls could come my way. Let me assure you that in the short time that I have been with your brother, there has been very little that was not discussed. Yes, I know all about Sonny and why he enlisted in the navy; and yes, I know why he decided that it would better for him to be away for four years. Oh, and yes, I know why Dominic left when his son was sixteen. To be frank, I am almost certain that if any one of us experienced the deceit that Dominic had to accept, we would have been gone way before a sixteenth birthday. To allay some of your fears for my future and well-being, I also come with baggage. I have a young daughter, and I am fourteen years younger than Dominic. My daughter loves him, and I wish I had the energy that he has. I want to thank you for your concern. It shows me that you care for me as one of your own. Thank you for that."

There was total silence in the room. One could hear a pin drop. Most of the people in the room shared hidden, surprised stares and looks. Gina had proved her point, but she saw an opportunity to press it even further: "Oh, by the way, when we first arrived and were exchanging 'hellos,' I heard most you refer to your brother as 'Jack.' I was wondering why."

Michael saw an opportunity to respond. He was still harboring ill feelings toward his brother: "Apparently, my brother didn't tell you everything. He was an excellent boxer in his younger days. He won a lot of fights. Most boxers, however, use a pseudonym when competing in the ring. He adopted the name of 'Jack Martin,' which was given to him by his wife, Marjorie. The name stuck, and the family, from that time on, always referred to him as 'Jack'."

"Oh, Michael. I didn't mean to imply that Dominic failed to tell me about his fighting days. He even told me that he managed a boxer who, unfortunately, met a tragic end. I guess he didn't feel that that it was important to discuss a name that was only connected to the boxing ring. However, after what he had been through in the ring, and the deceit that he experienced outside of the ring, I could understand why he wouldn't want to be reminded of the name or the deceitful person who labeled him with it. Thank you, Michael, for explaining, and I am sure that all of you will want to respect Dominic's wishes."

Once again, there was a pregnant pause in the activities. Gina had gotten up to the plate twice and had homered each time. Dominic was in awe of his girlfriend, and he saw a totally different side of her. She put people in their place without yelling, screaming or resorting to nasty or violent maneuvers. She was calm, cool and collected, and she was orally lethal.

Gina had taken the wind out of the sails of the attacking force, and the rest of the night was uneventful. Although Gina had met the opposition, mainly Alice, and had come out standing tall, Dominic knew that the Balaticco family would not forget the bashing that they were forced to endure at the hands of the young stranger. He knew that they would never be close to her, and at every chance, they would seek to hurt, embarrass, or disrespect her. Dominic was well aware of their thinking, and he would prepare Gina, as much as he could, for the onslaught yet to come. Unfortunately, it meant that there would be very few times that he and Gina would be involved in the Balaticco family gatherings, holidays, birthdays, and special events. He would miss those times, but he wasn't going to place Gina in harm's way. Presently, however, he wasn't exactly on good terms with some of his siblings, so invitations to those family gatherings would be few and far between for him anyway.

Chapter Thirty

The Family Home Meeting

It was obvious to Mary and her husband from what they saw crawling along the floor that the second dose of chemicals did not do the job. If Mary wanted to at least try to save her marriage, she would have to put the house up for sale and invest the monies from the sale into a new and better house. She made up her mind to sell but was at a loss as to how to tell the rest of the family that she was going to sell the home in which they had all grown up. The house had a special meaning to each sibling and specific memories that recalled endearing times. Her announcement had to be carefully structured so that they would all know that there was no other choice. It was, in fact, true that Mary had no other choice. She tried to correct the problem that came out of nowhere but dismally failed. They all knew what she and her family were going through, so, although painful, she was sure that her siblings would understand.

As Mary pondered her future and the ramifications of her problem, Dominic's parting words penetrated her thinking. What did he mean when he said that what she was experiencing could be a "gift from dad." It was perplexing for her brother to even bring up their father. She started to worry that Dominic might know more than she thought about their father's death. However, there was no way that he knew more than the rest of the family. She was sure that Frank never confided in Dominic, and she was the only other person who had firsthand knowledge. She was letting her mind go to places that really had no influence over the immediate problem. She put Dominic's words to the back of her mind and started to prepare her announcement to the rest of the family.

The first thing that Mary did was to discuss her plans with her husband, John. They met at a local diner because John didn't want to be anywhere near the house with those "creatures" crawling around in it. She described her plan to John and assumed that he would be ecstatic over the prospect of moving into a brand-new house that would probably be better than the one they were leaving. However, she was disappointed in his initial reaction. He had been living in an apartment that was close to their home, and he seemed to enjoy living alone without any of the nuances of family living. He had no responsibilities other than caring for himself. It seemed to Mary that John would be perfectly happy living the way he was and not sharing the responsibilities involving her or the children. The roach problem seemed to open pandora's box, and she wasn't sure, even with the lure of a new home, that she could close it.

John's reaction was less than lukewarm when he heard Mary's plan. She began to worry that not only did she lose the family home, but she might have lost a husband too. She was going to make sure that the house that they purchased would be impossible for John to walk away from. It had to be that good.

Right after the introductory meeting that Alice hosted for Dominic and Gina, she contacted Marjorie to let her know how things went. When Alice got Marjorie on the line, she could tell by her tone that her friend was not a happy camper: "What's up Marjorie? You sound like you're getting ready to go to a wake. Whatever it is, it can't be that bad."

"Alice, I have been replaced by someone who is fourteen years younger than me. Did you see how lively and bouncy she was? She was a kid compared to me."

"Marjorie, you're being foolish. Do you really think that a young, inexperienced kid could even come close to you? Jack is playing in the sandbox, and before long, the novelty of having a young playmate instead of a mature, good-looking lady will dissolve into boredom and disappointment. I can't say that Jack will come running to you asking to reunite, but he surely will regret his decision to leave."

"I don't know about that, Alice. Gina seemed pretty comfortable in her position and from what I am hearing, she is no novice in verbal warfare. I am sure that the fact that she can defend herself is attractive to Jack. She may be young, but she is not a pushover."

"Marjorie, you're giving her too much credit. I'll admit that she had a good day, but we will be pouncing on her every chance we get, and the cumulative effect will wear her down to the point that she will not want to continue catering to Jack."

"I hope you're right. Don't get me wrong, I don't want him back. I never loved him, but I hate to be replaced by someone that young and astute."

"Don't worry. Just leave it to me. I only met her once, and I already hate her guts. She'll rue the day that she took on the Balaticco family. I'll keep in touch, and cheer up!"

Marjorie was all alone in the house with Dominic leaving and her son in the navy. She had a lot of time to think. She regretted that Dominic had found out about her conversation with her girlfriend, but she really didn't want the relationship to continue. What she couldn't face was the fact that her one-time husband had found a younger person who was pretty and intelligent and who apparently made him happy. Marjorie was also shocked when she heard from Michael that Gina had verbally thrashed both him and Alice. Although Marjorie wasn't striving for any reunion between herself and Dominic, she wanted him to be as lonely and unhappy as she was. In her mind, it wasn't fair that he was enjoying life with a new person while she stayed at home alone and bored. At times, her self-pity was overwhelming. She felt that the only way she could introduce some angst and concern into Dominic's life was through his son. She decided to work on a strategy that would bring the happiness level in Dominic's life plummeting to a disastrous downfall.

Mary contacted the rest of the family and asked to meet with them. Alice, once again, offered her home as a meeting place, and the invitation emphasized that all the siblings should attend, if possible. Although Mary had asked Alice to host the meeting, she didn't disclose to Alice what the meeting was all about. Even when Alice asked, Mary said that it would be better if everyone found out at the same time. Alice was curious, but she didn't press the point. They would be getting together in just a few days, and she could wait that long to find out what was on Mary's mind.

Alice prepared some snacks and drinks for the meeting, and the Balaticco family was once again meeting for a family discussion. Dominic was one of the first family members to arrive, and he had a strong inkling as to why the meeting was called. The majority of the family had accepted the invitation, and they were now waiting with baited breath for Mary's announcement.

When everyone was settled, Mary thanked them for coming on such a short notice. She started her comments by emphasizing how important the meeting was. Her husband, John, sitting behind her, silently but emphatically nodded in obvious agreement.

"Let me start by telling you how difficult and tortuous these last few weeks have been. Some of you, or maybe all of you, know the problems that I have been having with my house, the house we all know so well. Not so long ago, I noticed what turned out to be a cockroach walking along the kitchen floor. We have never had any problem like that before, and I immediately contacted an exterminator to treat the problem. My husband is deathly allergic to any type of bug or insect, so I didn't hesitate to professionally treat the problem. In fact, until the problem was solved, John had to rent an apartment and stay there. Unfortunately, even after a second fumigation, the problem persisted. In an effort to strive for some sort of normalcy and to save my marriage, the only option left to me, now, is to sell the house."

There was absolute silence in the room. Heads turned to see the reactions of others at the meeting. What was evident was the fact that the majority of the people present had no idea that Mary was going to propose selling the house to which their childhood had been anchored. Following a lengthy pause, Mary spoke again: "I hope you all understand that I also have the same feelings that I see expressed on everyone's face. I too grew up in that house, but you have to realize that I have no other choice. I intend to use the monies that I realize from the sale to purchase another house and get our lives back on track. Dad left the house to me, and the decision, therefore, is mine.

Dominic listened carefully to Mary's plea for understanding. He also realized that he was probably the only one in the room who had read the fine print on the original paperwork involving the inheritance of the house. In fact, he was certain that Mary never even looked at the document. If she had, she wouldn't have found herself in such a compromising position, one which she was not yet aware of. Dad had left the house to Mary long before he realized that she and Frank were hastening his demise. He never had the wherewithal to change the paperwork, so the house went to Mary.

Following a lengthy discussion over other options that were really never realistic, the group agreed to the selling of the Balaticco house. Mary couldn't be happier and more relieved that the family accepted her proposal. Even John had a smile on his face which added to Mary's relief. Of course, Alice knew a real estate office which would handle the sale expeditiously and efficiently. She called the office in front of the group and made an appointment for the agent to visit the home the following day. Mary was thrilled that things were going so quickly. The faster she could sell the house, the quicker her life with John and the kids would get back on track. Mary thanked everyone, and the group started to disperse.

Dominic was one of the last family members to leave. Mary thanked him for helping her get through the emotional turmoil. He just nodded and didn't feel that it was the right time to burst Mary or John's bubble. That time would come, and Antonio would then rest in peace.

Chapter Thirty-One

Surprise, Surprise

Sonny had adapted well to the military way of life. He was assigned to a battleship and had already completed a Mediterranean cruise. He had taken leave in a number of foreign countries and totally enjoyed the new experiences and cultures. It was during one of these leaves that Sonny met a model who was working on a photo shoot in the Italian Riviera. The meeting came about purely by accident when Melissa slipped on an unknown liquid that had spread on the floor of a high-end night club. Sonny and some of his shipmates were sitting at a table when Melissa and two of her model friends came across the room in the company of their male escorts. Melissa lost her balance as a result of the slippery floor surface, and before she came face-to-face with terra firma, Sonny reacted to her shriek and put out his arm just in time to catch her before she landed on the unforgiving tile floor.

Melissa embarrassingly thanked the handsome sailor for his quick actions and was quick to acknowledge that she could have been badly hurt. Sonny could not believe his good luck by being in the right place at the right time. Melissa was a beautiful woman, and she was beholding to Sonny for saving her. She was so grateful that she asked if she and her friends could join Sonny and his comrades for drinks. The sailors couldn't say "yes" fast enough. So, for the rest of the evening, the models and the sailors shared drinks, laughs, and a generally good time.

For most of the evening, Sonny directed his attention toward Melissa. They exchanged small talk, and Sonny found out that Melissa was a Brooklyn girl who grew up not far from where he spent his childhood. She seemed to enjoy talking with Sonny as much as he enjoyed just being in her company. They seemed to really hit it off. Everyone at the table was having a good time, and no one wanted the evening to end. Contrary to popular belief, the models were down-to-earth regular people. They acted like they were just local women who happened to meet some men who were serving their country in the military. However, they were far from the ordinary local women. They were "to-die-for" beautiful, and the sailors were the envy of the entire club. The only ones in the club who were not having a good time were the male escorts who were charged with the overall safety of the visiting models. The escorts could not wait 'till the evening came to an end, and finally it did.

As the group simultaneously rose from the table to head back to their hotel and/or their ship, Sonny decided to risk all and ask for Melissa's contact number. He fully expected a calculated response as to why she couldn't give out her number. He actually asked on a whim, thinking "what do I have to lose?"

"Melissa, I had a great time talking with you and sharing drinks. I realize that the men you meet must consistently ask for your number, and now, I guess I can be counted among them. I don't expect that I will get it, but on the very slim chance that I might, it would be foolish for me not to ask." Sonny was waiting for the expected, practiced excuse why she couldn't reveal her number but was surprised and shocked when he heard her say: "I don't see anything in your hands with which to write."

Sonny wasn't sure that he heard her correctly, so he didn't react immediately. Melissa, not seeing Sonny reacting to her comment, repeated her statement. This time Sonny couldn't get a pen quick enough. He almost tackled one of the waiters who happened to be walking past and apologizing as he grabbed the pen from the waiter's shirt pocket, he turned to Melissa to show her that he had a writing instrument in hand. She smiled and because of the noise in the club, repeated her number twice. Sonny only had a napkin available to record the number, so he gently wrote Melissa's number on the weak surface of the very flimsy wiping paper. Melissa kissed him on the cheek and told him to "keep-in-touch." Sonny told her that he surely would.

Although the rest of his shipmates had a very good evening, none were successful in obtaining a contact number for a future meeting. They understood, but were in awe of the fact that Sonny was able to succeed where most men would have failed. He really piled it on by telling them that he had a certain charm that women could not resist. He continued by telling them that Melissa was just one of those women who fell into his web of addictive looks, personality and mature worldliness. His comrades-in-arms made noises to simulate that they were at the point of vomiting when they all broke out in laughter and congratulated their friend on a very successful night.

Although Sonny could not get to see Melissa, he kept in touch with her and asked for an address where he could send letters. She quickly responded to his request and Sonny wrote to her as often as he could. It was a long-distance relationship, and contrary to popular belief, one which seemed to grow stronger as time went on.

In one of the letters, Melissa informed Sonny that she was no longer modeling but was partnering with another woman in creating fashion for young women. She stated that she was residing back in Brooklyn, and that she traveled only twice a week to Manhattan. This was great news for Sonny. She was out of the very sometimes immoral and compromising modeling arena and concentrating on a business that would surely be lucrative. She was living a more normal life and that was great for Sonny to hear. In Sonny's mind, this news solidified his idea of pushing ahead with a more permanent relationship. At one time, he entertained the idea of making the navy a career, but now, he couldn't wait to get home. He still had about another eighteen months before his hitch was up, and those eighteen months now seemed like an eternity.

However, fate has a strange way of balancing life's choices. A short time after receiving Melissa's letter about changing careers, Sonny was working on the ship in a compartment adjacent to the engine room. As he approached the open engine room door, he was met with extreme heat and percussion that knocked him off his feet and into a valve that controlled the steam needed for power. There had been an explosion in the engine room where two sailors were killed, and two more severely injured. Sonny, who had not yet reached the engine room, was knocked unconscious and suffered injuries to his head and back. He was treated by the medic on board the ship but had to ultimately be transported to a military hospital for further medical evaluation.

Following an extended period in the hospital and enduring a barrage of tests, it was determined that Sonny suffered from a permanent concussion and could no longer remain in the military. He was given a Medical Honorable Discharge. He accepted this determination with mixed emotions. He wanted to be back home, but he didn't want to expeditiously be separated from the guys who had become his close allies, friends, and confidants. However, he had no choice. The navy made the decision, and he had to abide by it. So, Sonny would soon be on his way home. He decided that he wasn't going to tell anyone including his parents and hopefully his soon-to-be girlfriend that he was out of the navy and, once again, a civilian. He wanted his return to be an overwhelming surprise.

With the medical discharge, Sonny's time in the navy was cut short by about a full year. As he got closer to home, he realized that although he would miss his former shipmates, home was where he really wanted to be. Out of respect and duty, his first stop was his house where his mother had no idea that her son was permanently discharged from military duty. He didn't want to shock her, but he did want to surprise her. So, when he arrived at the front door, he didn't use his key to enter. He rang the bell. He heard his mother yell that she would be right there, and then the door opened.

Sonny heard a deafening yell, and felt a hug that could have injured a weaker man. Marjorie burst into tears and started asking one question right after another without waiting for any one of them to be answered. It was just a nervous reaction to a joyous and unanticipated surprise. Sonny succeeded in happily surprising his mother, who was relieved that he hadn't suffered any debilitating health-related problems from his experience. He stayed with his mom for a while and explained why he was discharged.

He had written to his mother about the model that he had met, and told her that he thought that she could be the one with whom he would spend the rest of his life. Of course, Marjorie warned him not to make any hasty judgments and to spend time getting to know her. He had agreed to do that, but now he told his mom that he wanted to surprise Melissa too. Marjorie understood and told Sonny that Melissa was a very lucky woman.

Sonny left his house and headed to the address that Melissa had given him. He borrowed his mom's car and got there in no time. Just as he approached Melissa's house, another car pulled up in front of the home and a young, middle-aged, good-looking guy, dressed to the nines, got out. He went up the front steps, and Sonny saw the front door open. Melissa ran into his waiting arms, and they both hugged for a long time. Sonny couldn't believe what he was witnessing. His heart sank, and the winds that had been inflating his sails of surprise quickly dissipated.

Sonny sat there in the car for a good while deciding whether or not to go ahead with his surprise plan. If he didn't ring the bell, he would never know who that man was. He had to know. Even if it meant that his dream becomes a nightmare, he was not leaving until he found out what relationship that man had with Melissa. He hesitantly exited the car and approached the front steps. He was there now, and there was no turning back. He negotiated the steps and rang the bell. When he heard footsteps approaching, he had a hard time restricting his urge to turn around and run.

Melissa opened the door and just froze. It was not exactly the reception for which Sonny was hoping. She said nothing and just stared at him in what could only be determined as disbelief. What went through Sonny's mind, however, was the thought that he might have interrupted a relationship in which Melissa was romantically involved. In the short span of seconds, the thoughts that flooded his consciousness were overwhelming. Fortunately, his stream of consciousness was interrupted as Melissa realized what she was seeing: "Sonny, what are you doing here. I can't believe that you're here." Melissa said it so matter of factly that Sonny was sure that his worst nightmare was about to come true. He was so taken aback with disbelief that he didn't know what to say nor what to do. He was just able to utter some words in a tone that was a notch above a whisper: "Hello, Melissa. I thought I'd surprise you, but apparently, I am the one who is surprised."

"No, no. I just can't believe that you're standing here. It is so good to see you." With that, Melissa finally hugged and kissed Sonny. Now he was totally confused, and it seemed that Melissa was playing her cards very close to the vest.

"Please come in. I want to introduce you to someone." Sonny felt like he was walking into the lion's den: "Sonny, this is Special Agent Greg Andersen. I owe him my life." Now Sonny was even more confused. He was just introduced to a federal agent to whom Melissa owes her life. What the hell was going on?

Following the introduction and handshake, Melissa turned to Sonny and told him that she needed to explain why the agent was there. She went on to tell him that her decision to leave modeling was influenced by an attempt at her kidnapping, and that if it wasn't for the actions of the special agent, the kidnapping would have been successful. She furthered explained that the agent had been injured, and that she told him that when he recuperated she wanted to invite him over for dinner. Greg Andersen was there accepting Melissa's invitation. She also told Sonny that she didn't tell him anything about the incident because she didn't want him to worry about her when he had to concentrate on so many other things.

Sonny felt like a fifty-pound weight was lifted off of his shoulders. He now understood why Melissa acted so strange when she first saw him. She had lied by omission and had felt totally guilty upon seeing him. The cloud in the room lifted and bright sunshine permeated the rest of the afternoon. His homecoming was more than welcomed by Melissa, and she couldn't wait to start getting serious about their future.

Just before the dinner party ended and Special Agent Andersen was getting ready to leave, he asked Sonny a specific question: "Did you say that your last name was 'Balaticco'?"

"Yes, that's right. Why do you ask?"

"Well, before I went into the State Department Protection Unit, I was assigned to the Department of Transportation as a special agent. Right before I transferred,

I was involved in taking down a hijacking team that had been stopping trailer trucks. If memory serves me correctly, I believe one of the arrestees, the leader of the pack, had the same last name as you. Is that a relative of yours?"

"Yes, I believe my uncle was arrested for hijacking."

The agent continued: "Before I left, I believe your Uncle Frank was about to disclose the names of the inside operators who facilitated all those crimes. If he did, he probably reduced his sentence and is out on the street now. He was doing the right thing as far as we are concerned, but I don't think he is going to get the 'good guy' award from organized crime."

After Andersen left, the mood turned into a serious and conflicting one. Sonny explained the roots of his family and assured Melissa that he had no part in any organized crime family. He told her that his father was a businessman in the garment industry, and that he would probably ask his father to introduce him to the industry. He also told her that he hardly saw or interacted with his uncle. For sure, he wanted nothing to do with his uncle. At this point, if what Special Agent Andersen said was true, Sonny knew that his Uncle Frank was a marked man. His life was sure to come to a tragic end, and Sonny did not want to become part of the collateral damage resulting from the mob's potential planned hit on his uncle. One does not betray the mob and live to tell about it!

Chapter Thirty-Two

The Hammer Finally Falls

The Balaticco house sold for the respectable amount of five hundred thousand dollars. Mary and her husband were gratified that they were able to see such a large profit from the sale. After the usual deductions and compromises for repairs, the final sale yielded approximately four hundred and fifty thousand dollars. It was a sum that Mary and John could easily apply to the purchase of a new home. When Mary and her husband announced the final sale to the rest of the family, Dominic asked that another family meeting be called. Not to delay their sister and her husband's search for a new residence, the meeting was arranged quickly, and once again, they all met at Alice's house.

Since it was Dominic's request to have the meeting, he was the one who welcomed everyone and announced that the reason for the meeting was to discuss the recent sale of the Balaticco house. The rest of the participants in the room just looked at each other confused as to why any further discussion about the sale was needed.

Dominic emphasized to the group that other than himself and Alice, the rest of the family were living a very modest existence. He further emphasized that he knew that they all could use additional monies to help out with everyday expenses and those future bills that would surely come their way as their children grew and needed to advance their educational levels. The group was still in doubt as to why Dominic wanted the meeting to take place. Even more confused and curious were Mary and her husband. They were ready to start their search for a new home and didn't appreciate Dominic delaying the process. Mary spoke up: "Jack, what's going on? We need to start looking for a new residence, and all you are doing is confusing everyone. Tell us what's on your mind and let John and I get on with our business."

"I'm sorry, Mary, if you feel that I'm delaying your progress, but I just don't want you to go ahead with your plans before you understand what has to be done. There are eight of us siblings in the Balaticco family, and six of us are surely impacted by the sale of the house." The group was still looking at Dominic with that confused stare.

"Me and Alice are leading very comfortable lives and are not in need of additional monies as are the rest of you."

Michael interrupted and yelled to Dominic to get to the point. He seemed annoyed that his brother was beating around the bush. However, knowing his brother, Michael was waiting for the devastating blow.

"Okay, Michael. I won't keep you or the rest of the family in suspense any longer."

Dominic had been enjoying the fact that he was keeping everyone on edge, especially Mary and her husband. But now that it was starting to get ugly, he decided to drop the bomb: "When our father gave Mary the house, he had papers drawn for Mary to sign, which she did. The papers indicated that he was leaving the house to Mary for her to maintain her residence thereat. However, the small print at the bottom of the page that, apparently no one cared to read, stipulated that if the house was ever sold, that the proceeds from that sale were to be divided among all of the remaining siblings. So, if the house was sold for a profit of four hundred and fifty thousand dollars, that amount must be divided among the eight of us. The total amount of the sale does not go to Mary alone. Mary would only get the same amount as all of us, which is fifty-six thousand, two hundred and fifty dollars."

There was total silence in the room. The siblings in the room were trying to digest what they had just heard. It was unbelievable to some and catastrophic to others. Following the pregnant pause, the room became a beehive of activity and voices. Many were just shouting questions at Dominic or requests to clarify what they all heard. Dominic raised his hand in an effort to calm the storm of questions and comments. When the yelling and screaming ceased, Dominic, once again, addressed the group: "Understand that I, for one, will not deprive any of you from getting your fair share. Although I could always use additional funds, I am not desperate for them. If anyone else would like to bow out of the cash give-away, then the divided amount would again increase."

Dominic looked directly at Alice when he commented on others refusing the allotted inheritance. He embarrassed her into stating that she, too, would not accept the money. So, the individual inheritance was increased to seventy-five thousand dollars. It was a tidy amount, but a dollar value that fell far short of what Mary and John thought that they were getting for a new house. If looks could kill, then Mary would have been responsible for Dominic's death. She rose from her seat and grabbed the document that Dominic had been waving in front of the group. She wanted to see the small print herself, and this time, she read it. All she kept doing was shaking her head in what could only be described as disbelief. In desperation, Mary addressed the group: "You all know the problems I have had. Are you just going to ignore that and take the money that John and I were going to use to buy a house? We cannot afford to invest in another house with only seventy-five thousand dollars to work with. Put yourselves in my place. Wouldn't you want others to understand how desperately you need the money?"

Unfortunately, Mary was preaching to her brothers and sisters, some of whom only lived in apartments. Mary was asking for them to understand that she wanted money to buy another house, something that the majority of them did not have. So, her pleas, for the most part, were falling on deaf ears.

Following her address to the others in the room, silence befell the meeting. Everyone was thinking about their own plight in life and figuring out how the newly found funds could make a difference in their everyday existence. Mary was failing to persuade anyone that she, John and her family needed the money more than they did. The way things looked, in addition to failing to gain their support, the pleas for a self-serving donation began to create schisms in the once closely bonded Balaticco family.

Seeing that Mary was not getting a positive response from her siblings, John rose from his chair, looked forlornly at his wife, and walked out of the meeting. He did not hesitate or turn as his wife called after him. John was gone, not only from the meeting, but more than likely from the marital relationship that he once shared with Mary.

Upon seeing John's exit, Dominic looked with satisfaction toward his sister, Mary; but while Dominic was looking at Mary, Alice was staring with disgust at Dominic. She knew that he had, in some way, orchestrated the entire attack on Mary's supposedly good fortune. Although Alice knew why Dominic was facilitating the takedown of his sister, she couldn't justify what she was witnessing. As she stood up and was about to address her siblings, Dominic pointedly spoke directly to her: "Alice, do you have something that you want to tell the rest of the group? Is there something that we're missing? Do you have anything that might change the outcome of the meeting? Please don't hold back. Tell us what's bothering you."

Dominic had goaded his sister, Alice, into complete silence. She was not about to tell her brother and sisters that Mary was complicit in their father's death. So, she just shook her head in a negative manner, and sat back down. When Alice retreated to her seat, Dominic asked the group if they had any questions. There was silence in the room until Mary got up and focused her comments directly at Dominic: "Well, Jack, you singlehandedly were able to destroy any semblance of improving my family's living conditions, and I'm almost certain that my husband, John, is preparing to leave for greener pastures. You have destroyed any chance that we might have had in purchasing a new home and, more significantly, you have, most likely, reduced me to the level of a single mom. I don't understand, Jack. Why would you do that?"

When Mary asked her question, Dominic looked over at Alice who shook her head in an effort to convince him not to reveal to the group what Mary and Frank had done. It took every ounce of restraint for Dominic not to announce to everyone what had taken place. He looked at Mary and said: "Mary, just because you lived in a house doesn't automatically mean that you should continue to do so.

People in this room are living in apartments and have to sacrifice to get through each day. I thought it only fair to follow our father's wishes and share whatever monies that came to the family. I am certain that the sharing of the profit will make life easier for the majority of people in this room. You may not be getting another house, but I am sure that you will be able to rent or purchase a suitable apartment for you and the kids."

Dominic turned to the rest of the group and said: "We will leave the disbursement of the funds in the hands of the lawyer, and if there are no more questions or comments, we can start heading out. Thanks for coming."

No one went over to console Mary as they left. It was a unanimous feeling that everyone should have benefitted from the sale of the house that had long been in the Balaticco family. Michael was the last one to leave, and he was able to corner Dominic before he left: "Jack,.." Dominic interrupted and reminded his younger brother that he didn't respond to that name any longer.

Michael continued: "Oh yeah, right. Dominic, you may have fooled the others in the family, but I know you pretty well. It is more than your affinity to fairness that influenced you to bring the small print to everyone's attention. Tell me what drove you to divulge something that would destroy one of your siblings and create an air of distrust among the rest."

"Michael, I did what I had to do. What some others in the family have done resulted in a finality that was outrageous and evil. I sought to balance the scales and bring others to a place that, unfortunately, doesn't deal in final endings, but creates a hardship that will impact the rest of their lives. And that, Michael, doesn't even bring the scale up to the midway point. So, what may have seemed to you like a disastrous undertaking, is merely a walk in the park when it comes to retribution. Know that I have done and seen these things through our father's eyes."

"If our father were alive, Jack, he would have never approved of what you did to one of our own."

"That's the point, Michael. He couldn't approve or disapprove of the actions because others have seen to it that he could not."

Dominic just stared at his brother, smiled and left him standing alone with only his private thoughts and assumptions. Michael did not want to assume the worst, but the negative thoughts flooding his consciousness were overpowering. His brother's implications should have been out of the realm of possibility, but, unfortunately, for Michael, reality looked him right in the face. He no longer wanted to deal in probabilities or possibilities. He wanted to know what drove his brother, Dominic, to attack with reckless abandon. If the influencing factor was that bad, it shouldn't be kept a secret. As far as Michael was concerned, Dominic wasn't going to be the self-appointed family member to mete out justice for a deed that probably affected the entire family. Michael was determined to know what drove Dominic to attack the well-being of one of his sisters. No matter the ramifications, Michael was going to find out.

Chapter Thirty-Three

The Balaticco Evolution

Time continued to pass, and the members of the Balaticco family saw a number of changes in their lives. Dominic proposed to Gina, and they married shortly thereafter. Sonny wasted no time in securing a lifetime with Melissa, and they married not long after Dominic tied the matrimonial knot. Mary moved to an apartment with her kids, and John filed for a divorce which was uncontested. Frank served his time in prison and contrary to what Special Agent Andersen had implied, Frank never divulged the inside operators. He was now back in the good graces of the crime family.

As with any family, change was inevitable as relationships solidified and parental obligations expanded with the increase of children born into the group. For instance, Sonny's wife, Melissa, was pregnant with their second child, and although Dominic had officially adopted Linda, his wife, Gina, was pregnant with the first product of their joint union. Their child, Matthew, was destined to be an only child even though he had a half-brother and a half-sister. However, although the Balaticco family saw many changes, one thing remained constant, Gina was still viewed as an outsider and was continuously and negatively compared to Dominic's first wife, the aggrieved Marjorie. Leading the never-ending attack was Alice who never forgave Gina for her responses during the original introductory meeting. She vowed that she would make life miserable for Gina and always make her feel like she was not wanted in the family. Alice was more focused on retaliation than her sisters were; however, they all followed Alice's lead and made sure that they never warmed up to Gina.

Marjorie, the object of the family's defensive actions, was a heavy smoker. She had upper respiratory problems that led her to many appointments with different doctors. She also had a hacking cough that would wake the dead. Having experienced the constant discomfort of congestive breathing and punishing periods of severe coughing, Marjorie was still not persuaded to stop or even reduce the amount of smoke she drew into her lungs. Even with the sincere and concerned pleas of her son, Sonny, she continued to tempt fate.

Although Marjorie was still a relatively young woman, her habit transformed her into a wrinkled, gasping-for-air, female who was never seen without a cigarette in her fingers or dangling from her mouth. One can only delay the inevitable for a limited amount of time, and for Marjorie, the time period had expired. She was diagnosed with lung cancer that quickly spread into other parts of her body. Her time on this earth quickly came to an end. Marjorie Balaticco met a painful but quick death.

The entire Balaticco family grieved for a long time, and although Gina had absolutely nothing to do with Marjorie's demise, her death served to amplify the negative feelings that Alice and the rest of the females had toward Dominic's wife. However, Gina expressed her condolences to the family and, in particular, to Sonny. She understood the bond between a son and his mother and was sincere in her regrets to him. Gina got along with Sonny, but Alice and the female hoard tried to keep Sonny and his wife under their wing. He was constantly hit with the negatives involving Gina and because of Alice's exaggerated closeness to him, a strong bond was never allowed to develop between Gina and Sonny. There was no obvious dislike, but their relationship could only be described as lukewarm.

In all the time that Dominic and Gina had been married, Sonny only visited a very few times. It was not that he wasn't welcomed, but the interaction always seemed strained. Also, when Alice found out that Sonny had visited with Dominic and Gina, he would have to justify why he acted so drastically. The female siblings in the family couldn't accept the fact that he was also visiting his father. All they could see was that Sonny was giving credibility to the idea of accepting Gina into the family. That's how bad it had gotten.

Gina decided that she would no longer put herself in a compromising position. So, whenever Dominic attended a Balaticco family event or just visited with the rest of the family, he did it alone. Dominic well understood his wife's decision and never pushed for her to accompany him. Although they didn't want any part of Gina, it incensed them more that Gina was not visiting and actually refusing to be in their company. Alice confronted Dominic on Gina's apparent decision and commented on how disrespectful it was for her to ignore the rest of the family. For fear that a major conflict would ensue between Dominic and his family, he only said that, in his opinion, the family did not make his wife feel comfortable. He quickly followed up with the fact that he did not want to discuss the issue any further. The conversation quickly ended.

Whenever Dominic visited with his sisters, they were usually at Alice's house. This was beneficial for Dominic, because around the corner from her house was a luncheonette where Sonny helped the owner, a long-time friend of the family. So, after visiting with the family on weekends, Dominic always made it his business to go to the luncheonette hoping to see Sonny. Most of the time, Sonny was there helping out, and father and son connected.

During the week, Sonny, through the influential contacts of his father, worked in a factory that focused mainly on producing shoulder pads and zippers. Sonny was well-liked by the owner, and there was talk that Sonny might be offered the prospect of buying into a partnership in the business which Sonny would have more than welcomed.

As Matthew got older, he went with his father to visit his family, and he always enjoyed visiting with his "cousin," Sonny. Since Dominic and Gina agreed to enroll their son in a Catholic elementary school, they thought better than to let him know that his parents were divorcees who both had children from previous marriages. So, as far as Matthew was concerned, Sonny was his cousin, and Linda was his sister with the same mother and father as he. This misinformed relationship lasted for many years, and although Sonny and Linda knew the truth, Matthew labored under the falsehood that was compounded throughout his childhood, adolescence and even for part of his adult life. In fact, later on in years, Linda died never knowing that her brother, Matthew, knew the truth regarding their relationship, a relationship that she foolishly thought would suffer if Matthew ever found out that she had a different father than he.

Frank had been out of prison, and as promised, he was appointed to a very well-paying position as the Promotions Director of the New York City Convention Center. Frank never gave up the two detectives who facilitated the hijacking operation. He took the fall and was rewarded for his silence.

However, it still bothered him that he never found out who made that anonymous call to the police that resulted in his incarceration. He had asked his brother, Dominic, to help answer the nagging question, but he hadn't come up with a name. Now with his enhanced freedom, he decided, also at the behest of the mob, to investigate the situation himself, and he vowed that when he found out who it was, the individual would regret ever picking up the phone. It had been too long a period of time for the traitor to still enjoy life.

The mob did not like loose ends, and the fact that this individual still roamed free was a loose end. If the person squealed to the police about the hijacking operation, then it was possible that this individual could do the same thing regarding other matters. It was far too long a period of time that the caller had not been identified. The mob told Frank to make the identity of the squealer his primary goal. Frank had no problem with following the orders because he had a personal matter of approximately five years to square with the anonymous caller.

Frank made it his business to meet with Dominic to catch up on what had occurred while he was gone. Although Dominic had visited his brother in prison a number of times, the visits were authorized for only a brief few minutes, and one could only discuss a limited amount of topics. Although in Frank's case, the discussion usually centered around the identity of the person who landed him in prison.

In a most recent meeting with his brother, Dominic, Frank asked where he had left off in finding the identity of the anonymous caller: "Hey Jack, excuse me, I forgot that 'Jack' is off-limits. Dominic, I know you continued to investigate the anonymous caller's identity for me, but how close are you to actually getting a name? It seems to me that by now you should have easily discovered who made the call. Or is it that you know who it is, and you do not want to reveal the identity for fear that the person might meet a tragic end. Dominic, don't mess with me. If you know who it is, tell me."

"No Frank. I've exhausted all of my options, and I am not any closer to discovering who made the call. Whoever it is has a great cover and a support team which has, apparently, pulled out all of the stops to protect him."

"Hey Dom. You said 'him.' Do you know for sure that it is a 'him' and not a 'her'?"

"Frank, it's just a figure of speech. It could be a female, but I would figure that only a male with an axe to grind would have the balls to make a call that in the end might put his life at risk."

"That's a good point, Dom. I guess that I'll have to start looking at individuals who have something against me. That might turn out to be a long list, but I know that I can depend on you to continue to help out."

"No problem, Frank."

"One last thing before we split. When you're in prison, you have a lot of time to think about things. What did you mean when you said, 'it may be a gift from dad'."

For a moment, Dominic was caught by surprise, but he was always one who could think on his feet. He answered Frank with a determined tone: "Oh, I even forgot that I said that, but, at the time, it came to my mind that your incarceration, nasty as prison is, could have saved your life. And the gift from dad was his saving you from a future that might have included a premature end."

"You know, Dominic. You were always the thinker, the philosopher in the family. I would have never thought of that. I'm glad I asked."

Frank seemed satisfied with Dominic's answer, but Dominic knew, by Frank's tone, that his brother was only temporarily satisfied. Dominic knew that the comment that had bothered Frank would come up again. But then, it would probably be accompanied by an accusation that might just result in a retaliatory act which included physical harm or even death.

Chapter Thirty-Four

Michael's Interrogation

Michael was close to his sister, Alice, so he decided to start delving into the secret that his brother, Dominic, was holding close to his chest. She was the youngest female sibling, and he was the youngest male. They had that natural common bond between them, and Michael was going to capitalize on that commonality to find out anything he could from Alice. He wasn't sure that she knew what Dominic had in his back pocket, but if she did know, he would worm it out of her. Michael just couldn't believe what Dominic had done to Mary and her family. He didn't accept his brother's excuse of "fairness" as the reason why he had brought up the conditions mandated in the "small print." Michael knew his brother, and he was sure it was more than what Dominic had proposed.

Alice was glad to hear from her brother, Michael. She always got along with him and was closer to him than any of her other brothers. She was even more thrilled when Michael mentioned that he wanted to get together with her for a drink or two. She readily agreed, and they made arrangements to meet after work. He didn't mention to her that the purpose of the meeting was to interrogate her as to whatever she knew about Dominic's secret. He framed the meeting in the fact that they had not gotten together for a while, and that he missed chatting with her. Alice was so receptive to the idea of meeting Michael that she offered to meet for dinner instead of just drinks, and she said that it would be her treat. Michael couldn't resist the offer of a free meal and the additional time it would afford him to play detective and find out what she knew, if anything.

Alice had chosen a local restaurant that had a reputation for the best steaks in the area and the strongest drinks in the city. It was a great location, and its reputation brought many people to its tables. Without a reservation, even on a weekday night, there was a strong possibility that a person would have to go elsewhere to satisfy his appetite because the place would undoubtedly be at capacity. Alice had made reservations, and after a brief wait, they were escorted to one of the prime tables in the restaurant.

The evening was going along so well that Michael almost forgot why he wanted to meet with Alice in the first place. They were enjoying some after dinner drinks when Michael decided to broach the subject that had influenced him to contact Alice: "Hey Alice, what did you think about the meeting that Dominic called regarding the sale of the house?"

"I don't know, Michael. I have mixed feelings about the whole thing."

"Yeah, me too. I can't believe that Dominic introduced a document that he knew would destroy Mary and her family. I know he mentioned that it wouldn't be fair to the rest of us if Mary kept all the money, but I have a real hard time thinking fairness was the only reason he did what he did. It's not like Dominic to do something like that without at least speaking to Mary first. I don't know, Alice. Am I way off-base on this?"

Before Alice responded to Michael's question, she took a long swallow of alcoholic support: "Yeah, Michael, I was also surprised at how coldly Dominic introduced the problem. It was like he didn't care who got hurt. He was determined to make his point, and you're right, he's not like that."

"You know, Alice. It almost seemed like he had something against Mary to devastate her like that. Has Dominic mentioned anything to you that would have you believe that our brother is out to get Mary?"

The more they spoke about the situation, the more nervous Alice got, and her nervousness was beginning to become obvious to Michael. Being an intelligent and perceptive individual, he asked Alice if she was okay. She hesitated for a long moment, and Michael saw tears starting to well up in her eyes. Michael knew that he had hit upon something, so he persisted with some more pointed questions and the discussion.

Although Alice heard Michael, she kept looking down and not responding, Now, for sure, Michael knew that she too might be protecting the same secret. He was not going to leave this time without the secret being revealed.

"What's the matter, Alice? You say that you're okay, but you're definitely not acting it. If you know something, you have to tell me. Do you know why Dominic attacked Mary and John?"

"Michael, it is killing me, but I can't tell you anything. There are things that both Dominic and I know that would definitely impact our family bond. In fact, the impact would be so great that it would change our relationships forever. I can't be the one who initiates something like that."

Alice's refusal only pushed Michael harder to find out what was so significant that its revelation could potentially dissolve a family bond that was second to none. No, Michael was not going to let her get away with whetting his appetite and then just killing it with an "I can't."

"Alice, are you kidding me? What do you mean 'I can't'? You cannot keep something that you deem so important locked away from the rest of the family who will be affected by it. If it's not you, sooner or later, someone will find out, and that someone will know that you knew it all the time and kept it to yourself. How is that going to look to the rest of us? Whatever it is, we have to know. We've worked things out before as a family, and we will work this out too. I can see that it is burning a hole in your stomach. You shouldn't have to deal with this alone. Let us help. Let me help. I will find out one way or the other, so please make it as easy as possible for me. If you want, and for a while, I will keep whatever you tell me in the strictest confidence. However, the time will come when either you or I will have to let the rest of the family know what is going on. Alice, once you unburden yourself, you will feel a lot better. Let me help."

Alice no longer just had tears in her eyes. The tears were flowing down her face. More than anything, she wanted to tell Michael all she knew, but the ramifications of her confession would have such far-reaching effects on the family that they presented a formidable obstacle to her revealing all. She was trying to figure out how she could just tell Michael a small part of what she knew, but she realized that there was no small part.

"Okay, Michael, but for now, just keep this between us. I really don't want the rest of the family to know, and I especially don't want Dominic to know that I betrayed his confidence."

"I understand, Alice, but like I said, sooner or later the rest of the family has to know. I'll keep it between us for now."

Just as Michael finished speaking, he heard Alice's pager going off. When Alice looked down, she saw Dominic's number on the screen. She hesitated. She didn't want to speak to Dominic now, but the impulse to answer was so strong that before she knew it, she was on the payphone saying "hello."

"Hey Alice, how are you doing? I called Michael's house, and his wife told me that he was out having dinner with you. Is it a special occasion? Did I miss something?"

"No, Jack. I hadn't seen Michael in a while, and we just wanted to re-connect. You know, a reunion of the babies in the family."

"Yeah, that's cute. It might be a reunion for you, Alice, but I'm pretty sure it's something else for Michael. He has been quite inquisitive lately, and I would bet my bottom dollar that he was the one who suggested that the two of you meet. Be careful, Alice. Once you tell Michael anything, there is a good possibility that Frank will also know. I know he is our brother, but if Frank finds out that we know what he and Mary did, our safety would be put at great peril. In other words, it is not beyond Frank to hurt either one of us."

"I understand Dominic, but I can't talk right now. I'm with Michael, and we are enjoying a nice dinner. I will talk to you soon."

Michael was aware that Dominic had paged his sister, and he had heard a small part of the conversation, but Michael wanted to know more, so he asked Alice: "What did Dominic have to say?"

"Nothing much. I think he wanted to talk to you since he had called your house. Denise told him that we were meeting for dinner. I guess it wasn't important. He'll probably catch up with you later."

"Alice, if he wanted to talk to me, why did he page you? That doesn't make sense. Did he possibly want to warn you not to share the secret that the two of you are apparently harboring? Alice, you were going to tell me what's bothering you. I'm listening."

"Michael, you're very close to Frank. I'm nervous about your reaction, and more importantly, Frank's. At some time in the future, I will confide in you, but for now, we should call it an evening."

"Alice, you've made it worse. For Dominic's own good, he'd better come clean. Frank is the wrong person to mess around with. Maybe it would be a good idea if Frank speaks directly to Dominic. He will get the secret out of him. I will have to give him a call."

"Don't do that, Michael! He has murdered once, and I'm sure he is capable of doing it again."

"What are you talking about?"

Alice said nothing more. She got up and left, ignoring the pleas to "wait" behind her. She had indeed made it worse. She told Michael that their brother was capable of killing since he had already done it before. As Alice left the restaurant , all she could think of was: "What have I done?"

Chapter Thirty-Five

The Truth Revealed

As a result of Alice's comments, Michael was left in a quandary. He couldn't believe what he had heard. He knew that Frank was a tough guy, but he never thought that his brother would ever resort to taking a life. Maybe, Alice was wrong. How could she know such a thing? Michael could not leave her accusation just floating in thin air. It bothered him so much that he decided to confront Frank. How better to debunk such an idea than to go to the subject of the accusation. He was close enough to Frank to bring up such a serious subject. Although he was closer to his brother prior to the arrest, he still spoke to him on a somewhat regular basis. So, it wouldn't be unusual for Michael to want to speak with Frank. However, because this was such a serious subject, Michael wanted to meet with him face-to-face and discuss Alice's comments.

Michael contacted his brother, Frank, and asked to meet with him. Frank was most receptive to his younger brother's invitation and told Michael that he looked forward to getting together. When Frank asked Michael if there was something in particular that he wanted to talk about, Michael just glossed over the question and said something to the effect that they hadn't gotten together in a long while. Frank seemed to be satisfied with the answer and told Michael when he would be available. Michael agreed to the time and date, and couldn't wait to clear up the misconception that Alice apparently held.

Frank had been dedicating the majority of his free time to investigating why and who made the anonymous call to the police the day that the arrests went down. Now, it was not just his desire to solve the mystery but also the command of the crime family to find out who put their members and the operation of the family in jeopardy. They had been waiting a long time for the answer, but they felt that since Frank was the one who was personally impacted by the betrayal, he should be the one to find the person and administer mob justice. Out of character, they waited for a long time for Frank to become available. Or was it a way to teach Frank a valuable lesson?

Although Michael had what seemed like a legitimate excuse for not being with the hijack group on the day of the arrests, Frank wondered if the excuse was engineered without Michael's knowledge. He was almost certain that Michael had no involvement in any planned absence, but it was all to coincidental for Frank to just accept the whole idea on face value. Frank decided to pay a friendly visit to the pastor of the church where Michael worshipped. Frank knew that Michael had close ties to the pastor and the church and was sure that the pastor would have wanted to help Michael, if he could.

Frank would couch his visit and questions in the context of helping his brother. Additionally, Frank wanted to settle his conscience before his meeting date with Michael. The pastor could easily shed some light on the situation. By the pastor's answers, tone and body language, Frank would be able to tell if the pastor was being totally truthful. If he was demonstrating what Frank thought to be less than an honest response to the questions, Frank would resort to other measures to exact the truth.

Without phoning in advance for an appointment, as was the procedure for a visit to the rectory, Frank just showed up at the front door and rang the bell. A young woman, who apparently was the receptionist, answered the door and asked Frank if she could help him. Frank was his charming self and told the woman that he was a personal friend of the pastor and Michael Balaticco's brother. The receptionist recognized the Balaticco name and escorted Frank into the waiting room. Before long, Pastor Patrick McLoughlin came into the room and greeted Frank.

"Hello, Frank. I haven't seen you in a very long time. I hope you are here for me to hear your confession so that you can receive the sacraments." The pastor was sarcastically friendly and knew that a confession was definitely not the reason why Michael's brother was visiting. There could be a number of reasons, but Pastor McLoughlin was almost positive that a confession was not one of them.

"No, pastor. Maybe some other time, but now I wanted to speak to you about the incident that occurred some years ago when my brother, Michael, was, unfortunately, locked in a room in the basement of the church."

"Oh yes, I remember it. Unfortunately, the door to the room is very old, and it slammed closed before either one of us could get to it. The room itself is an old room and hardly used, so finding the key to the door was a difficult and time-consuming task. It took me quite a while before I found the key. Poor Michael became a prisoner in the room. I felt very bad about the whole thing, and I apologized to Michael who was very good about the whole thing."

"Pastor, could we go into the church basement so that I could take a look at the room and the door?"

"Certainly, Frank. Is there a particular reason that after all this time, you are interested in what happened to Michael on that day?"

"I would have come sooner, Pastor, but I was away for a while. I only recently returned. So, even though it has been a while, I would like to take a look."

"Is Michael concerned about something that occurred in the basement that day?"

"No, Pastor. In fact, Michael doesn't even know that I am here."

When Frank mentioned that Michael was unaware of his brother's visit, red flags went up for the pastor. Pastor McLoughlin was well aware of Frank's sorted past and reputation. He became worried that Frank wanted to know if Michael's temporary imprisonment was an accident or a planned activity. However, the pastor knew that there was no way that he was going to convince Frank to take his word that it was an unfortunate accident. Apparently, Frank wanted to determine that for himself. The Pastor was starting to get nervous, and beads of sweat were appearing on his brow. He did not want Frank to see how edgy he was, so he stayed in front of Frank as he lead Michael's brother to the basement of the church.

They walked to the church and went down the basement stairs. As expected, Frank commented on how dingy and dirty the basement was. Even with the filth and dim lighting, Frank began to notice that the pastor was a little edgy as they approached the basement, and even more nervous as they came to the room.

"Here it is, Frank. As you can see, the room and the door, are especially very old and in need of repair. When the door closed, it was impossible to open it without the key."

Frank went over to the door and tried swinging it. There was a lot of resistance indicating to Frank that the door, most likely, didn't swing closed by itself. After testing the door, Frank spoke to the pastor: "Wow, Pastor. Did you see how difficult it was for me to move the door? It was almost frozen in place, and I had to use some strong elbow grease to swing it one way or the other. Are you sure that the door swung closed by itself even though I could hardly move it?"

Pastor McLoughlin, who was standing behind Frank, hesitated in his response but maintained that the door did, indeed, swing closed on its own. Frank nodded and turned back to inspecting the door. With no indication whatsoever, Frank quickly turned back to the pastor swinging his right hand up and squarely across the face of the pastor. It was so severe and such a shock that the blow almost landed the pastor on the floor.

"Pastor, I do not want to bring down the wrath of God on myself, but I will risk my relationship with him in an effort to get the truth out of you. Do you understand?"

The pastor just stayed quiet which aggravated Frank, so in an attempt to loosen the pastor's lips, another vicious slap landed on Pastor McLoughlin's face. It was such a pointed blow that blood was now flowing from the pastor's mouth.

"Pastor, I will ask you again. Was the door closing an accident or a plan to keep Michael from leaving? Don't make it hard on yourself. I will ultimately get the truth even if I have to beat it out of you."

Frank raised his hand again to plant another blow, but before Frank could follow through, the pastor raised his hand in submission: "Wait, Frank. It was more than an accident. We wanted Michael to be delayed for a time."

"Well, Pastor. You're being smart now. Do you know why someone wanted to stop Michael from leaving?"

"No, Frank. I have no idea."

Frank started to raise his hand mocking another slap, but the pastor told him that he could beat him near to death, but he did not know the reason why.

"Okay, Pastor. Now the big question. Who asked you to delay my brother's exit? Don't hesitate. Just say it right out."

"Dominic asked me to do it."

There was deafening silence in the basement, and Frank, almost not believing it, repeated what the pastor had said: "Dominic told you to keep Michael here. Is that what you are saying?"

The pastor just nodded. Frank was beside himself, and on the way out of the basement, he walked passed the pastor, thanked him, and unexpectedly punched him square in the face. It sent the pastor reeling to the floor. Frank bent over the priest and whispered: "That's because you colluded with my brother against me. You should thank your God that I didn't kill you. No, on second thought, you should be thanking me!"

Pastor McLoughlin stumbled into the rectory and told the alarmed receptionist to call Dominic Balaticco. The situation and the physical assault having taken its total negative effect on him, the pastor collapsed to the floor losing consciousness.

Chapter Thirty-Six

A Sibling's Revenge

Instead of calling Dominic, the pastor's receptionist immediately called for an ambulance and then dialed Michael Balaticco, someone with whom she was more familiar than Dominic. She explained to Michael that his brother, Frank, had visited with the pastor, and they were examining the basement room in which he had been imprisoned years ago. At first, Michael was surprised to learn that Frank went to the rectory. Frank hadn't even been near the church in years, but when the receptionist further explained what Frank wanted to do, red flags went up. Michael was incensed when he learned that Frank raised his hands to the pastor. If his brother did that without any remorse, Michael didn't want to think about what Frank might do to someone who really betrayed him.

After hearing all of the details from the receptionist, Michael immediately left his house and drove to the emergency room at the nearby hospital. When he got there, it looked like a basement sale at Macy's. He had never seen a hospital so busy. It took him a while before he was able to locate the cubicle where Pastor McLoughlin had been placed. He was lying in bed looking like he just lost a ten-round fight with a champion. He could hardly open his eyes, and he appeared to be fighting to stay conscious. The doctor gave him a preliminary evaluation and ordered drugs to reduce some of the apparent pain that the pastor was experiencing. A nurse was applying some topical ointment on the bruises that were swelling to the point that his face looked disfigured. While Michael stood by the cubicle waiting for the nurse to finish, a police officer came to talk to the pastor.

The nurse having finished with her application, the police officer entered the cubicle and told the patient why he was there: "Hello, Pastor Mcloughlin, I am Police Officer Jacobs. I know that you are uncomfortable and in some pain, but I have to ask you a couple of questions. I'll be as quick as I can."

The pastor nodded as well as he could, and the officer began his questioning. Officer Jacobs asked the pastor what happened, and was told that the patient fell down the basement stairs of the church. When the officer more closely examined the injuries that the pastor sustained, he told him that the injuries did not look like they were the result of a fall down the stairs. The pastor insisted that his injuries were the result of a clumsy accident and nothing more. Although the officer still doubted that the pastor was the victim of a fall, he did not persist on focusing on the cause of the injuries. The officer asked if there were any witnesses to the fall or if anyone responded to the basement. The pastor responded negatively and told the officer that he was able to get to his office where the receptionist called for an ambulance. Officer Jacobs saw that Pastor McLoughlin was tiring, so he ended his comments and left his business card for reference if the pastor needed it.

During the entire time that the officer was there, Michael was standing within earshot right outside of the cubicle. When the officer left, Michael entered and approached Pastor McLoughlin: "Okay, Pastor. I heard what you told the Police Officer, now what's the real story?"

"Michael, are you implying that I was less than truthful."

"Yeah, Pastor. I am saying that the drugs must have affected your train of thought, and you confused an assault with an accident. Let's not beat around the bush. What happened?"

"Well, Michael. Your brother, Frank, paid me a visit. He wanted to know what happened some years ago when you were trapped inside the room in the church basement. I told him that the door accidentally closed and locked you in, but he had a different idea about what occurred."

"Pastor, was it an accident or was it done intentionally?"

"After convincing me to tell the absolute truth, I confessed to Frank that I intentionally allowed the door to close and lock. Although I told him what he apparently wanted to hear, he was not happy that I was part of a scheme to delay your leaving. He let me know how unhappy he was."

"Pastor, I can't believe that Frank would hurt you like that, and I definitely do not agree with what he did. However, I also can't believe that you intentionally locked me in that room. Why?"

"Michael, I have my suspicions, but I really do not know why I was asked to do it."

"Let me guess, Pastor. My brother, Dominic, was the one who asked you to cooperate with him. Is that right?"

Pastor Mcloughlin slowly nodded in the affirmative and followed with: "I am so sorry, Michael. I meant no harm by doing what I did. Knowing Dominic, I just assumed that it was for something good. Maybe, I was wrong."

Michael was disappointed but not surprised. He knew that in Dominic's eyes, it was for something good. However, it made Michael look very suspect when he wasn't there with Frank the one time that the police showed up. Michael was sure now that Dominic had betrayed his brother and made the anonymous call to the police. More than that, Frank now also knew that Dominic was the one who was responsible for taking years from his life.

Michael was not sure what Frank would do, but he was absolutely certain that Frank was not going to let the fact that Dominic betrayed him just roll off his back. Now, even more so, the statement that Alice had made about Frank already taking a life became of paramount concern for Michael. Would Frank ever consider going to the extreme with Dominic? Michael didn't want to answer that question, and he couldn't let that happen. His next stop was Dominic's house.

Frank Balaticco was livid. His own brother turned against him and caused him to be imprisoned for those years. Brother or not, Dominic was going to pay for what he did. Wasting no time, Frank brought what he had learned to the attention of his mob boss, Tony Delfiato. The boss didn't seem that surprised to learn who the culprit was. It had become obvious to him when he considered that what occurred years ago saved the youngest brother in the Balaticco family from arrest. However he waited to retaliate because he wanted Dominic's brother, Frank, to take care of their family matters. After Delfiato heard the news, he calmly asked Frank what he was going to do about it. Frank just commented that he would take care of it. That was not good enough for the boss, so he asked again: "What do you mean you'll take care of it? Tell me how you will take care of it."

Frank was not ready to discuss the subject any further because he hadn't decided what he was going to do. However, staying silent wasn't an option: "Mr. Delfiato, I will put a hurting on him that he will never forget."

"You understand, Frank, that you must make an example of your brother. Others must know that they can never go against our family or any one of our members. A hurting is not sufficient. Do you understand?"

Frank looked at him and realized that the boss was dictating his brother's demise. Frank was really upset and concerned over what Dominic had done, but he didn't think that it warranted Dominic's death. If he didn't think so, and he was the one who ultimately went to prison because of it, why would anyone else think that the ultimate price should be paid? However, Frank learned a long time ago not to question the dictates of the family boss. He felt like he was in a "no-win" situation. In fact, he was.

When Michael left the hospital, he immediately found a phone and called Dominic's house. His wife, Gina, answered the home phone: "Hello Michael. What can I do for you?" Gina came right to the point with everyone in her husband's family. She knew that there was no love lost, so why pretend that there were good feelings amongst them?

"Hello Gina. I am trying to find Dominic, but he is nowhere to be found. Is he at home?"

"No Michael, I believe that he said he was going to stop by Alice's house before coming home. Why? Is there a problem?"

"No not really. I just wanted to speak to him about something. I'll try again to find him. Thanks, Gina. By the way, how are the kids? They've probably grown inches since the last time I saw them."

"Michael they're always here. If you wanted to see them, all you have to do is stop by." Gina learned as time passed, not to give an inch when it came to the Balaticco family, and she didn't.

"I know, Gina. I will make it my business to visit soon."

Showing total disregard as whether he visited on not, Gina answered with the irritating: "Whatever."

When Frank left Mr. Delfiato, his initial feeling that the boss would have been pleased, quickly dissipated as Frank realized that the boss was ordering Dominic's death. Frank also realized that if he didn't do it, or he took too long in carrying out the mandate, two things would occur: one, Mr. Delfiato would find someone else to whack Dominic, and two, that because of the delay or refusal, Frank would also become a target. Although he hated what his brother did to him, he felt that he wasn't going to be able to kill his own blood even though he had expedited his father's demise. He had to figure out a way to save his brother, but appease the boss of the crime family.

Dominic decided to surprise Alice and visit her after work. He wanted to talk to her about letting the rest of the family know what they knew. It was getting too difficult to keep the secret, and he was almost sure that Michael would soon find out on his own. However, when he rang the doorbell, to his surprise, his brother, Michael, answered the door.

"Well hello, Dominic. I've been trying to get in touch with you. I'm glad you're here."

"Why, Michael? Was there something you wanted to talk to me about?"

"I don't want to talk to you about anything. I just want to tell you that the cat is out of the bag. Both Frank and I both know that you made the call to the police as well as arranging for my safety in the confines of the church basement those years ago. To say the least, Frank is on the warpath. He beat the truth out of the church pastor, and I'm sure that he is looking for you. In fact, according to the pastor, who is presently in the hospital thanks to Frank, he is so mad that he could kill."

"Well, Michael. I'm glad you brought that up." Alice looked at Dominic knowing that he was about to tell all. That was something that she was not yet ready for, but harboring the secret had become extremely stressful. She said nothing and just listened.

Dominic continued: "Michael, I have no doubt that Frank could kill me. In fact, as Alice and I both know, he has killed before."

Michael interrupted his brother and tried to downplay whatever Dominic was going to say about Frank. He suggested that Frank probably had to kill some low life who was more than likely threatening to kill him.

"No Michael. That 'lowlife' was your father who only wanted the best for his children, but both Mary and Frank decided that Antonio was taking too long to die. So, to gain their advantage, they slowly poisoned him until his body gave out."

Michael's eyes were popping, and he couldn't believe what he was hearing. Since the body had been cremated, Michael wanted to know how Alice and Dominic found out about the alleged poisoning. Dominic explained that Alice overheard Mary speaking to Frank, and she heard Mary mention the killing of their father. Dominic then reached into his pocket and pulled out a piece of wrinkled paper that he always carried with him. He gave it to Michael and told him to read it. After Michael was told what the English translation was, Dominic explained that the message was given to him by Mary as Antonio lay on his death bed. Michael was stunned and at a loss for words.

"Michael, just so you know it all. I was the one who orchestrated the cockroach infestation in Mary's house, and I was one the one who called the police. No, I couldn't kill either Frank or Mary, but I wanted some sort of justice. I wanted them to suffer for dad's untimely death. So, I caused some grief to come into both of their lives, but it in no way balances the scale regarding our father's death"

Just as Dominic finished speaking, Michael's pager activated. When he looked at the screen, he saw Frank's number appear. He showed Dominic and Alice the screen and then called Frank: "Hello, Frank. What's cooking?"

"I am looking for that two faced piece of shit who turned on me and you. He is going to suffer for what he did. I may need your help. You don't have a problem with that do you?"

Michael had turned up the phone volume so that they all heard what Frank said. Dominic nodded to Michael to answer in the affirmative to Frank's request: "No, Frank, I have no problem. Whatever you need."

"Michael, I might need a pine box!"

Chapter Thirty-Seven

A Wife's Surprise

Michael agreed to meet with his brother, Frank. When Frank hung up, Michael turned to Dominic in a quandary as to what to do next. Dominic calmly said that he would meet with Frank and square things away. Michael looked at him as if he were crazy and said: "Did you hear what Frank said? He wants to put you in a pine box. Dominic, he wants you dead."

Alice, who had been quiet most of the time, chimed in: "Dominic, Michael is right. We all know how ruthless Frank can be. You are not going to be able to talk your way out of this. You get him riled enough, and I believe he will kill you."

Dominic knew that Frank was capable of murder, but Frank also had an Achilles' heel, his wife Colleen. Dominic would work his magic through Colleen who would surely want to convince her husband that any type of violence was not the way to settle things. Colleen was a God-fearing individual who always saw the good in others. Dominic got along well with her, and was depending on that relationship to buffer Frank's plans. Dominic explained the situation to both Michael and Alice who at the very least were doubtful that anyone, including Colleen, could divert Frank from his rage-influenced vendetta against his older brother.

Although Michael worked with and was close to his brother, Frank, he did not want to see Dominic get hurt. Michael may not have agreed with what Dominic had done, but he understood why he did it. Because of Dominic's actions, Michael did not have an arrest record, and he spent no time in jail. It was obvious that Michael benefitted by his brother's actions, but another family member, Frank, suffered from them. It was difficult for Michael to reconcile between the two, but the fact that Dominic could be physically harmed or even killed overshadowed Michael's thinking. He decided that he was willing to help Dominic in any way that he could.

Dominic asked Michael to call Frank and arrange for a meeting right away. When Frank agreed to leave for the meeting, Dominic would head for Frank's house and speak with Colleen. Michael got on the phone and dialed Frank's home phone number. Frank heard the edginess in Michael's voice and asked him if everything was okay. After assuring his brother that everything was fine, Frank agreed to meet with

Michael at the local bar in about an hour. However, before they disconnected, Frank, once again, asked Michael if there was something bothering him. Michael insisted that he had no problems and just wanted to talk. Frank didn't persist and repeated that he would meet Michael in the bar in about an hour. They hung up, and Michael took a deep sigh of relief.

In reality, however, Michael did want to speak to his brother, Frank. Although his pleas might fall on deaf ears, he was going to try to convince Frank that getting back at Dominic with aggravated violence would prove nothing. He would tell Frank that he no longer had to interact with Dominic, and the dismissiveness would truly hurt Dominic. Dominic would have to live with the fact that he lost a connection to a brother with whom he would never deal with again. Although it all sounded very convincing to Michael, but he wasn't sure that his idea would control the flames of revenge that ignited in Frank and lessen the hate that Frank was harboring toward his older brother.

Again, Alice spoke up, and this time told Dominic that she was going to go with him to Frank's house. She was closer to Colleen than Dominic was, and she might have a greater influence over Colleen's feelings and cooperation. At first, Dominic balked at the idea of Alice possibly putting herself in harm's way, but she convinced Dominic that she was already there. She explained to Dominic that once Frank found out that she was the one who initially instigated the whole situation, he would hold her in the same light in which he was holding Dominic. In her words, "the damage was already done." She was quite convincing, and Dominic yielded to her argument.

The time for the meeting arrived, and as Michael left to see Frank, both Alice and Dominic left to meet with Colleen. Dominic approached Frank's house very cautiously wanting to make certain that his brother had left for his meeting with Michael. It would be a disaster to arrive at Frank's home while he was still there. He checked and saw that Frank's car was gone. That was a good sign. However, he and Alice still approached with caution. You couldn't be too careful when it came to Frank and his potential bad temper. Dominic rang the doorbell, and, as expected, Colleen answered the door.

Colleen was surprised to see Alice standing at the door with Dominic behind her. She was so surprised that she didn't immediately greet them. When the shock subsided, she welcomed both of them into the house. Her son was at a friend's house, so Colleen was alone in the house. That made things even easier for the two apprehensive guests.

Colleen finally greeted them: "Wow, this is a surprise. You just missed Frank. He went out to meet with Michael. I can page him and let him know that the two of you are here and maybe he'll get Michael to come back home with him." They both answered "no" so quickly and simultaneously that it alarmed Colleen. She looked at them with questioning eyes and commented: "Wow, that was a resounding 'no.' By the way the two of you are acting, your visit isn't geared to delivering good news. Please tell me what's on your mind."

As planned, Alice was the first to speak: "Colleen you're right. We are not here to celebrate or share good news. We are here to ask for your cooperation and support in dealing with a very serious matter. To get to the point, something that Dominic has done caused Frank some hardship, and he wants Dominic to pay for it. However, Frank is so incensed by what occurred that his blind rage could influence him to resort to violence. We need your help in persuading Frank that there are options other than violence."

Colleen interrupted: "Before you gone on, Alice. What could Dominic have done that brought Frank to such a state?"

Dominic now answered: "Colleen, I don't know exactly how much you know about your husband's activities. However, many times, he acts outside of the limits that the law allows. He, unfortunately, got Michael involved in similar activities, and I made certain that when things backfired, Michael was not going to be a part of the results. Furthermore, my actions led to Frank spending time in a state correctional facility for approximately five years. He recently found out that it was I who had a part in the police response that resulted in his arrest and incarceration. That's the story in a nutshell."

Apparently, although Colleen was somewhat aware of Frank's vocation in life and his stay with the State, she was shocked to hear that Dominic squealed on his brother and sent him to prison. After mentally digesting some of what Dominic had said, she spoke: "I am shocked to hear that

Frank is still involved in illegal activities, and even more shocked to hear that you facilitated Frank's imprisonment. I suppose that you are hear now to ask that I try and diffuse some of Frank's anger in an effort to better secure your safety. Is that correct?"

Alice saw that Colleen's ire was rising, so she stepped in: "Colleen we are not telling you this only to secure our safety, but to make sure that Frank doesn't do something foolish that jeopardizes his future like he did once before."

"Alice, I understand why Dominic is here, but what is your involvement with Frank?"

"Colleen, this is going to be difficult for you to accept, but Frank was an integral part in expediting my father's death."

Colleen yelled out: "What are you talking about?"

Before you yell out and interrupt me again, let me finish, and maybe I'll answer some of you questions: "There was a time when I paid a surprise visit to my sister, Mary. When I arrived at her house, she was on the phone and unaware that I was in the house. I didn't want to disturb her, so I just waited until she was through with the phone call. While I waited, I overheard her telling the person on the other end, Frank, that she was nervous about what they did to Antonio. She and Frank hastened my father's death by poisoning him. It was I, then, who told Dominic what I knew. Dominic also had evidence that Mary and Frank plotted

Antonio's death. Dominic made it his business to exact revenge for our father's demise."

At that point, Dominic went into his pants pocket and presented the wrinkled piece of paper that his father, through Mary, had given him. Colleen looked at the Italian words and Dominic quickly translated what they said. Colleen just shook her head in disbelief. She looked up and waved the paper in front of her as she asked: "Does Frank know that you have this? Does he know that Alice heard the conversation? Does anyone else in the family know what has occurred?"

Dominic answered: "I am not sure if everyone knows, but I am sure that some are suspicious. I don't know what Frank knows, but now that you know, Colleen, can we count on your help?"

Before Colleen could give an answer, the front door opened and standing in the doorway was Frank and Michael. One could see that Frank was enraged that Dominic brought his wife into the fray. With a defined threatening tone, he spoke to Dominic: "You made a bad mistake by coming here, but apparently you are prone to bad mistakes. I am going to make certain that you never make a bad mistake again."

Frank pulled out a gun and pointed it directly at Dominic.

Chapter Thirty-Eight

Double Trouble

It was obvious to Dominic and Alice that even though Michael seemed to agree with everything that Dominic had said, he contacted Frank as soon as he left Alice's house. He told Frank what his brother and sister were planning to do, so Frank developed his own strategy and gave Alice and Dominic enough rope to hang themselves. Frank's plan worked exceptionally well and caught his brother and sister totally by surprise. Even Frank's wife was shocked to see her husband appear at the front door.

Frank shook the gun at Dominic and said: "I should blow you away right now. I spent years of my life rotting away in a prison because of you. You don't deserve to live."

Dominic thought at that point that the final sound that he would ever hear would be the gunshot, but before Frank pulled the trigger, Dominic spoke up: "I deserve to die? You got it wrong, Frank. You're the one who killed our father. You're the one who should die. Spending some years in prison doesn't absolve you from the fact that you committed murder. Both you and Mary will get your just desserts when you have to go before your maker."

Instead of Dominic trying to calm things, his comments aggravated the situation even more. Michael looked at Dominic as if to say: "Do you really want to die?" Colleen was trying to comprehend all that was taking place, but she became quite concerned when she saw the hate and determination in her husband's eyes. She reached her tipping point, however, when she saw Frank pointing the gun at his brother. Knowing her husband well, she feared that he was at the point of no return and was ready to shoot. Following Dominic's comments that encouraged more violence than dissuaded Frank's ambitions, Colleen stepped in front of Dominic and questioned Frank: "Frank, is Dominic telling the truth? Did you and Mary conspire to end Antonio's life? I can't believe that you would do something like that."

Colleen's intervention slowed the terror train, and Frank's attention was now directed toward his wife: "Colleen, my father was dying anyway. Because of his existence, my rising up the promotional ladder was delayed. He had made enemies who didn't forget what he had done. So, all I did was hasten his entry into the afterlife. It helped both me and Mary. I didn't kill someone who wasn't already dying."

Colleen looked at him as if she never really knew him. The disbelief and disappointment on her face indicated that she was not accepting Frank's flawed logic.

"You are telling me that you killed your father so that you could get a step up at work, and so Mary could, apparently, inherit the house. Is that what you are telling me, Frank? If it is, then I really don't know who you are, and I can't stay with someone who puts his own advantage before a human life. And here you are pointing a gun at your brother threatening to kill again. How could I have been so wrong about you? Get out, Frank. Get out!"

Michael witnessed Colleen's tirade and approached Frank. He spoke calmly to him and tried to usher him out of the house. Frank didn't respond, and everyone waited with baited breath for Frank's next move. Colleen had acted totally out of character, and she sent the room into an unpredictable silence.

Michael saw the opportunity to coax the gun out of Frank's hand or, at least, lower it to the floor. As Michael placed his hand on the weapon, Frank violently drew it away and accidentally discharged a round. Everyone was stunned, but none more so than Michael who lay on the floor with a bullet wound to his abdomen. Michael was in severe pain and bleeding profusely. As Dominic rushed to Michael's side, Alice immediately called for an ambulance. Both Colleen and Frank stood stunned at what had developed. They didn't move until they heard Alice speaking to the police dispatcher. They then both realized that once the police were involved, Frank was going to be charged with a crime, and more than likely sent back to prison for, at the very least, a parole violation.

Frank bent down to look at how badly Michael was wounded, and he told Michael how sorry he was. He then rose to look at Colleen who was stoically still standing in place. It seemed as if she was in the state of shock. Frank went over to her and told her how sorry he was for everything. He then whispered to her that he had to leave before the police arrived. Colleen still stayed mute and didn't respond in any noticeable way. Frank kissed her on the cheek, made eye contact with the rest of his siblings in the room and fled. The police, for sure, would label Frank Balaticco as a fugitive from the law.

As Frank drove away from the house, he heard the sirens in the distance. He had failed in his mission to take down his brother, Dominic, and had placed Michael's life in jeopardy. It is common knowledge that a wound to the abdomen, many times, results in a fatality. Frank prayed that it would not be the case, this time. As he thought about his brother Michael, he also thought about the ramifications for failing to get the job done as the mob wanted. He knew that Dominic's life would still be in jeopardy for his betrayal, but he also knew that his own life was in peril because of the failure. Frank realized that there was only one way to wipe the slate clean, and it would free both him and his brother,

Dominic, from the pursuit of organized crime. Frank had to eliminate the source of all his worries, Tony Delfiato, the one who would now hold a vendetta against the Balaticco brothers. It would not be easy, and he knew that the risk could result in his extinction, but there was no other way. He wanted to set things straight, and it was the only way that he knew how.

Dominic contacted his son, Sonny, and told him what had happened. He asked Sonny to meet Alice and the others at the hospital. He told his son that he was going to try and find Frank before the police did, and before Frank did something stupid. Sonny was distressed but followed his father's wishes and headed for the hospital. By the time Sonny got there, his Uncle Michael was in the operating room, and the rest of the family was participating in that tortuous waiting game that hospitals forced on families. Some were in tears and others were in shock, but all were concerned for Michael's well-being.

The only one who was obvious by her absence was Mary. There had been a message left on Mary's answering machine, and the family was shocked that Mary had not yet responded. Her apartment was close to the hospital, and everyone thought that she would be the first one to arrive. As the time passed, there was still no word from Mary, and the rest of the family became concerned; however, no one wanted to leave before they found out about Michael. So, they all stayed concerned but did nothing about it.

Mary heard the message and was very worried about her brother. She started thinking about what might have led to Michael being shot, and she thought about how she contributed to her father's death, something that constantly weighed heavy on her mind. The news of Michael's wound and the actions of Frank compounded the guilt that she already felt. Her kids were with their dad, and she was alone. She wanted and needed relief from the overwhelming grief, so she poured herself a large glass of wine and found what she believed was the sharpest knife in the kitchen draw. She gulped the wine and headed for the bathroom.

She sat on the floor with her back against the wall. Next to her were the almost empty glass of wine and the kitchen knife. She grabbed the glass and finished off the remaining wine. She was satisfied with the warm feeling it generated in her, and it calmed some of the nervousness that she was feeling. She took the knife, looked at it pensively and applied its sharp edge to her wrist. She repeated the application to her other wrist, and closed her eyes waiting for effects of unconsciousness to relieve the pangs of her never-ending guilt.

When John, Mary's ex-husband, returned to Mary's apartment with the kids, he rang the doorbell but got no response. He waited and rang it again, and again there was no answer. One of the children had a key, and he utilized it to open the door. Although John did not like going into the apartment without Mary knowing that he was there, he accompanied the children into the apartment and called out for Mary. He again heard no response and figured that she was out of the apartment, either shopping or taking care of other errands. However, it was odd that she wasn't there because she always made it a point to be home when he brought the kids back. He decided to wait with the kids until Mary got back. Just as he sat on the couch and started to relax, he heard an ear-piercing scream. He ran to the bathroom from where the scream had originated and saw his child screaming and shaking. Mary was sitting on the floor framed in a pool of blood.

The wait for the Balaticco family wasn't getting any easier and the only distraction they had available was the activity in the emergency room. It had gotten even busier than when they first arrived. As they looked at the many patients arriving by ambulance and seeking emergency treatment, Sonny saw a familiar face. John, Mary's ex-husband, was running alongside of a gurney that was being ushered into the emergency treatment room. John had to stop at the emergency room treatment doors, and he watched as Mary was wheeled in for potential life-saving treatment.

Sonny was sure it was John and went over to him to find out what was happening. John explained the entire scenario to Sonny, and he relayed the abbreviated version to the rest of the family who couldn't believe their ears. Mary had lost a lot of blood, and there was no guarantee that the doctors could save her. If nerves hadn't already been frayed, this new development put the edginess over the top. There was a possibility that the Balaticco family could lose two of their own in one day.

This sort of stuff happened to other people, or in tragic Hollywood movies, not to them. Although there was shock and tears, there was no speaking. The Balaticco family had fallen into a mode of deafening silence. But if one looked closely, the lips of each and every family member were moving in silent prayer asking for God's mercy.

Chapter Thirty-Nine

The Cousins

After contacting Tony Delfiato and lying to him about the success of his mission, Frank asked to see him regarding some other concerns that he had. Delfiato, satisfied that Frank had successfully carried out the execution contract, agreed to meet with Frank. Frank was already on his way to see the crime boss. He was going to see him whether Tony Delfiato agreed to it or not. Frank would have no problem getting past the stationary manikin-like guard at the entrance to the back room of the restaurant supply store. If Frank had to, he would use whatever means necessary to get to Tony Delfiato, including his silenced-equipped semi-automatic sidearm. He did not want to harm anyone including the boss, but he knew that there was no other way to, at least temporarily, secure the safety of his brother, Dominic.

Dominic was in a panic to try and find his brother, Frank, before he did something radical that jeopardized his life. Dominic could only think of one location where Frank might be heading. Dominic knew where Tony Delfiato stayed during the day; so, he headed to Manhattan where the restaurant supply store was located. If Frank was not there, then Dominic would have no idea where his brother went. When Dominic pulled up across the street from the store, he saw his brother's car parked by the entrance. Although he was gratified that he found his brother, he was at a loss as to his next move. He knew that getting in to see the mob boss would be no easy task, and that he would have to get by the rather large individual who was always there securing the back-room entrance.

Dominic decided that he was going to play it by ear. He exited his car and headed toward the store entrance. He was good at thinking on his feet, and he was sure that he could convince the guard that his visit with Tony Delfiato was a necessity. He entered the store, nodded to the salesperson behind the counter, and without hesitating headed to the back room which was out of site from the front of the store. Dominic's worries about getting past the formidable guard barrier became moot when he saw the large man lying motionless in a pool of blood. Apparently, Frank had violently persuaded the guard to let him in to see the boss.

Dominic was taken aback by the site of the dead man and hesitated going any further. However, he heard his brother's voice coming from the back room; so, without further delay, Dominic barged into the room. Frank, not knowing who was attempting to save the boss, turned his weapon on the intruder only to see his brother, Dominic, standing before him. When Frank realized who had entered, he quickly turned his weapon back on to Delfiato. Frank had reacted so quickly that Delfiato did not have enough time to get to the weapon that he always secreted somewhere in the back room. His attention back on Delfiato and still menacing the boss, he questioned why his brother was there: "Dominic, what the hell are you doing here? You're going to get yourself killed. Get out of here."

"Can't do that, Frank. I can't let you continue to kill people. There has to be another way. If you kill him, you will be as bad as he is. That's not what you want, is it?"

"You don't really understand, Dominic. I am as bad as he. Now, get out of here before you get yourself killed!"

Just as Frank finished his warning to his brother, a figure appeared behind Dominic. The unknown individual pushed Dominic aside and fired at Frank. The impact caused Frank to involuntarily pull the trigger, and the discharged round landed squarely in the chest of Tony Delfiato. It was a fatal round, and the crime boss quickly fell to the floor and expired. Dominic dove to the floor and grabbed the gun that Frank had been holding but was now laying on the floor. In one continuous motion, Dominic turned and was able to get off a shot that felled the intruder, the salesperson from the front of the store. Dominic reached for his brother and cradled him. Frank looked up at Dominic and whispered "I'm sorry" before he took his last breath.

The Balaticco family's wait was over. They had lost a bother and a sister within minutes of each other. Mary lost an excessive amount of blood, and she was unconscious to the end. The impact of the round that entered Michael's abdomen did too much damage to his internal organs. He died on the operating table. There was no comforting the rest of the family. They sobbed and kept asking God "why?" No one in the family, at that time in the hospital, realized or knew that they had lost not two of their family, but three.

Dominic didn't know that he was the only surviving brother left in the Balaticco family, and if he didn't get out of the location that he was in, his survival could very well be in question. He was alone with three bodies, one of which was his brother's. Unfortunately, he had to make his escape and leave his brother there. He did not want to do that, but there was no other choice. He grabbed the gun with his prints on it and ran. From a safe distance away, he made an anonymous call to the police from a nearby payphone that fortunately was in working order. He informed the dispatcher that he had heard gunshots coming from the restaurant equipment store.

Following a police investigation, Dominic was certain that the detectives would ultimately be notifying the Balaticco family about the death of one of their members. He was also certain that since there were no eyewitnesses to the carnage, it would be difficult to connect him to what went down in the backroom. When he ended the call to the police, Dominic quickly drove back to the hospital where he was hoping to get some good news.

Not wanting to alarm anyone regarding the blood that stained his clothing, Dominic went to his shop which was closed on the weekend. He washed and got rid of the stained garments. Fortunately, he always kept a change of clothes in his office. After quickly dressing, he headed to the hospital to find out about Michael and Mary.

When Dominic arrived at the hospital, the family was still there and grieving about their loss. He didn't have to ask about his brother or sister. It was apparent what had happened. He also grieved about the loss, but it was somewhat mitigated by the thought about two of his siblings who had taken a life. God had rained down justice and took the lives of those who took a life. However, in Dominic's mind, there was no justice when it came to Michael's death. Dominic, unfortunately had only one avenue in which to seek comfort regarding Michael's demise, and that was to call to mind the adage that he had heard many times: "God works in strange ways."

The Balaticco family had been decimated, and instead of the family growing closer, they became loners, each dealing with the needs of their own immediate families. It stayed that way for a very long time. They still kept in contact with one another, but the contacts were few and far between, and because of the attitude of the adults in the family, their offspring had an even more distant relationship. Cousins very rarely saw each other, and there was no bond to draw them together. After a while, the relationships deteriorated so badly that relatives lost track of one another.

The Balaticco family had drifted so far apart that when Dominic and Gina's son, Matthew, reached his twenty-first birthday and became a police officer, no one in the family even knew about it. However, fate has a strange way of setting things back on track. Two of the graduates in Matthew's unusually large academy class turned out to be his cousins. They, of course, had different last names since they had adopted the surname of their fathers, but the cousins recognized the Balaticco name.

Matthew and his two cousins renewed their dormant and almost non-existent relationships and started hanging out together. This newly rejuvenated association planted the seeds that would surely result in a bond that had been weakened for a very long time by a lack of meaningful communication. Apparently, family ties had not been totally destroyed but were just suspended waiting for fate to fertilize another generation of growth.

Unfortunately, Dominic Balaticco never got to see that bond grow into an even stronger connection than the original family could have imagined. Dominic had been the victim of a drive-by shooting that ended the storied past of a one-time, up-and-coming boxer named Jack Martin. It took the life of the oldest and only surviving son of the Antonio Balaticco family. Anthony Delfiato Jr. had avenged his father's death and was the living reminder of the brutality associated with organized crime where the mob never forgives or forgets.

In his final fight, the fight for his life, Jack Martin, for the first and only time, went down for the count!

Epilogue

For All Eternity

Prior to Dominic's tragic and untimely death, the Balaticco family reunions seemed to revolve around getting together at wakes and funerals. It was at one of these wakes that Alice was holding court, so to speak, with her nieces and nephews. Included in the group were Sonny and Matthew. As Alice continued speaking with the group, she happened to prejudicially and intentionally mention that of all of her nephews, Sonny was her favorite. No one was shocked by her statement, but it caused one in the group to start thinking about relationships. It had never occurred to Matthew before, but he now looked differently at Sonny. His thinking focused on Sonny's parents. If Sonny was a cousin then who were his parents? There has to be an aunt and uncle.

Matthew didn't ask anyone at the wake about the relationship, but the unanswered question bothered him, and he decided that he would query his parents about the mystery when they arrived home.

Following dinner that evening, Matthew posed the question to both his mother and father. The question caused grief and surprise to rise up on the faces of his parents.

"Mom, Dad, when Aunt Alice said that Sonny was her favorite nephew, it caused me to think about his parents, my aunt and uncle. I couldn't come up with the names of his parents. I am confused. Who are Sonny's parents?"

As Dominic and Gina heard Matthew, they realized that they could no longer keep the truth from their son. They also knew that Alice, who was aware of the fact that Matthew's parents were harboring a secret, intentionally brought the subject to light. It was another way that Alice could get back at Gina, who she still considered an intruder rather than a family member.

Gina was the first to respond to Matthew's query: "Matthew, you were going to catholic schools, and we didn't want to put you in a compromising position. Your dad was married once before, and as a result of that marriage, he had a son. That son is Sonny. He is not your cousin, but your half-brother."

For the first time that he could remember, he had ill-feelings toward his parents. In his mind, there was no valid reason for them to have deceived him for so long in this way.

"How could you guys keep that from me. I have a brother, not a cousin. I would have liked to get to know my brother better. I had to learn the truth from an aunt who probably said what she said so that I would question the relationship. She succeeded."

Matthew asked to see the birth certificate and other papers relating to what he had just learned. Without thinking and in an effort to show Matthew that they were not hiding any additional information, Dominic found the family birth files and gave it to his son. As Matthew carefully examined the paperwork, he suddenly stopped and looked up at his parents and said: "What is this?"

In Matthew's hands were papers that showed that Linda, Matthew's sister, was born with a different last name than his.

Matthew inquired: "What's this? Why did Linda have a different last name?"

Gina responded: "Matthew, I was also married before. Linda is a product of that marriage. Your dad legally adopted her when she was still very young. In fact, she knows no one else but Dominic as her father. However, she knows that she is adopted and feared that if you knew the truth that you would feel differently toward her. That is why we never said anything to you."

Matthew was in shock and disappointedly spoke to his parents: "I can't believe that the two of you have been living a lie for so long. It was so unfair to keep something like this from me. I am afraid to ask, but is there anything else I should know? Are you wanted by the law? Did you kill anyone? Do I have any other brothers or sisters floating around?"

Dominic and Gina treated these questions as rhetorical and didn't answer. However, Dominic said: "I am sorry that we hurt you, but we thought we were doing the right thing in protecting you. You now know everything."

Matthew just looked at his parents with a distressed and incredulous stare. He left the room and said nothing else.

It was shortly after the unexpected revelation that Dominic was ruthlessly gunned down on a Brooklyn Street. By the very nature of this tragic event, the impact of Matthew's parents' previous deception mellowed out of necessity since there was no one left who could be negatively affected.

Unfortunately, for Matthew, he never really got a chance to get closer to his brother, Sonny; and he looked at his sister with even more admiration now than he had before. Unfortunately, both Sonny and Linda had been victims of an aggressive cancer, and their time on earth was severely diminished. However, Matthew had been able to let his brother know that he regretted his parents' decision which deprived them both of getting closer; and although Matthew knew the truth about Linda, he never let her know. She died in the comfort of thinking that he was still unaware of the truth.

Matthew Balaticco, all of a sudden, was an only child whose father met a tragic end, and whose mother strove 'till the day she died to make up for a mistake that could never be remedied.

Matthew strayed from his aunts and uncles on his father's side and was only close to his Aunt Alice when he visited his mom and dad at the cemetery. Alice was laid to rest in a gravesite only twenty feet from where Dominic and Gina had been buried.

It was ironic that two women who had no love for each other, would spend their eternal interment facing each other just twenty feet apart. If one listened closely, one could hear Dominic continuously attempting to mediate a compromise that, in life, could never be reached and unfortunately seemed to remain that way in the boundlessness of never-ending eternity.

It wasn't a "Hades" dictated by a supreme being, but poor Dominic was experiencing his own private hell. For as much as he tried, it became tortuously obvious to him that he could not bring about a meeting of the minds between Alice and Gina. He was relegated to and accepted the fact that eternity in the present situation, one that most likely would never change, disregarded the intent of the quote which read: "Rest-in-Peace." There would be no rest, and apparently, no peace!

Acknowledgements

Once again, I must thank my wife who is my unofficial partner in all of my writings. It is she who I constantly ask for suggestions, and it is she who often gives me that elusive word that I just can't capture. In addition to proofreading, she offers constructive criticism that makes the read a more enjoyable escape. Thank you, **Chinch**. The very next person who I'd like to mention is my daughter who pushed me into looking to the past and putting it into print. Without her constant encouragement, I may not have taken on such an endeavor. She also volunteers to proof read my manuscripts and point out areas that may need some correction. Thank you, **Donna**. My two granddaughters, **Lauryn** and **Jenna**, have shown a keen interest in the family history and especially in those incidents of the past that may have seemed out of bounds. I tried to answer some of their inquiries, and I thank them both for their never-ending curiosity. My son has been involved in helping me with my creative ventures, and is always there to read the manuscript before publication. He has a keen eye which helps prevent me from offering a flawed product. Thank you, again, **Marty**. **Dave Manzolillo** has once again created a cover that draws in potential readers to find out what is beyond his intriguing artistry. You never let me down. Thank you. As always, I want to thank Mr. **Avi Gvili** for ushering me along and having the confidence in me to publish my work, and my editor, Ms. **Aliyah Manuel** for always being there to assist with problems that assuredly arise. Thank you both. Finally, I want to thank my **Mom** and **Dad** who actually lived through circumstances that could possibly resemble those portrayed in this book. Thank you for being as strong as you were, and know that you are sorely missed every day.

www.ingramcontent.com/pod-product-compliance
Lightning Source LLC
Chambersburg PA
CBHW041745010726
47507CB00008B/291